PEN
HUG YOURSELF:
EMPOWERMENT STORIES FOR TEENAGERS

Vinitha is an award-winning author and editor who also paints and writes poetry. An ex-journalist and columnist, Vinitha has written over thirty books for children. Her stories are part of CBSE and ICSE curriculum. Her book *Ammu and the Sparrows* won the Neev Literature Award 2021 and is a part of Parag Honour List, while *Jamini Roy's Unbroken Lines* has received much critical acclaim. A scholarship she won at Hedgebrooke's Writers in Residence Program has led her to write her first not-for-children book—a food memoir.

ADVANCE PRAISE FOR THE BOOK

'*Hug Yourself* is an intervention—a gentle, friendly and loving shout out to yourself just for being, not for looking or doing. This wonderful bouquet of vulnerabilities and victories is that cool older sibling/mentor/imaginary friend (if that's your jam) that hears you out sans judgement as you come of age.'—Mallika Dua, digital creator, comedian and actor

'Having grown up fat, without the reaffirming body positivity movement or media representation that we have today, I truly believed I was the only person in the world to feel as alone and isolated as I did. It took years of community building, unlearning, and a relentless, sometimes painful reckoning with childhood trauma to undo that damage. Growing up bullied or othered does a strange thing to a person. It makes you feel like you're screaming for help into a void and nothing, no one replies. That itself is a special kind of grief. If I had found something like *Hug Yourself* then—a collective, loud, unfettered call to action—I would have felt less angry at myself and the world. I hope this book reaches a young person who needs it just like I did, and I hope she finds a small reflection of herself in it.'—Harnidh Kaur, investor, poet and feminist

HUG YOURSELF

Body Positivity and Empowerment Stories for Teenagers

Edited by Vinitha

FOREWORD BY MALLIKA DUA

PENGUIN BOOKS

An imprint of Penguin Random House

PENGUIN BOOKS

Penguin Books is an imprint of the Penguin Random House group of companies whose addresses can be found at global.penguinrandomhouse.com

Published by Penguin Random House India Pvt. Ltd
4th Floor, Capital Tower 1, MG Road,
Gurugram 122 002, Haryana, India

Penguin
Random House
India

First published in Penguin Books by Penguin Random House India 2024

Anthology copyright © Penguin Random House India 2024

Copyright for individual stories vests with their respective authors

All rights reserved

10 9 8 7 6 5 4 3 2 1

This is a work of fiction. Names, characters, places and incidents are either the product of the author's imagination or are used fictitiously and any resemblance to any actual person, living or dead, events or locales is entirely coincidental.

Please note that no part of this book may be used or reproduced in any manner for the purpose of training artificial intelligence technologies or systems.

ISBN 9780143470557

Book design by Gina Mary James
Typeset in Sabon LT Std by Manipal Technologies Limited, Manipal
Printed at Thomson Press India Ltd, New Delhi

This book is sold subject to the condition that it shall not, by way of trade or otherwise, be lent, resold, hired out, or otherwise circulated without the publisher's prior consent in any form of binding or cover other than that in which it is published and without a similar condition including this condition being imposed on the subsequent purchaser.

www.penguin.co.in

MIX
Paper | Supporting
responsible forestry
FSC® C010615

CONTENTS

Foreword — vii
Editor's Note — xi

1. Fifty Shades of Grey (Hair) — 1
   Neha Singh

2. Fatty Batty and the Fat Demons — 12
   Anuja Chandramouli

3. Hills and Valleys of Nangeli — 28
   Vidya Nesarikar

4. Second Skin — 34
   Vibha Batra

5. Ms Jasmine Jaw — 47
   Aditi De

6. Hair Today, Gone Tomorrow — 62
   Harshikaa Udasi

CONTENTS

7. Beauty and the Beast — 77
   Vinitha

8. The Smell of Earth — 85
   Shals Mahajan

9. Darken My Kajal — 89
   Suha Riyaz Khopatkar

10. Colour Bar — 112
    Smita Vyas Kumar

11. My Mane Concern — 128
    Ratna Manucha

12. Raw — 140
    Janani Balaji

13. Life in the Headlines — 145
    Nandini Nayar

14. The Most Beautiful Girl in The World — 162
    Priyanka Sinha Jha

15. This Isn't Fair — 182
    Santhini Govindan

16. Sinking into My Skin — 196
    Rajani Thindiath

Acknowledgements — 207

FOREWORD

Growing up, there was no term of endearment that my parents didn't use for me, and there was no term of disgust or shame that I didn't use for myself. I'd like to believe it's been a few years since I have, well, grown up, and I'd be lying if I said I don't shame myself even today. I just shamed myself for writing this trite, cringey opening. Cringe opening by a cringe girl with a cringe double chin and cringe, frizzy hair. I don't really believe that deep down. I've just written this the way I speak to and about myself. What an unkind way to speak to and about someone who does so much for me every day. I wouldn't let anyone speak to me the way I speak to me, and yet . . . I do.

If you're bored enough in life to read a foreword, you'll agree with me as I take the liberty to declare that I know I'm not the only one who talks to herself like this. I hope you don't agree with me. If you do, hug yourself.

FOREWORD

My foremost thought upon reading the manuscript was a loud 'WTF! Why didn't I have this when I was a teenager?' Then I got over it, wiped my cathartic tears and began writing. *Hug Yourself* is an intervention—a gentle, friendly, loving shout out to yourself just for being, not for looking or doing. This wonderful bouquet of vulnerabilities and victories is that cool older sibling/mentor/imaginary friend (if that's your jam) that hears you out sans judgement as you come of age.

I'm so glad kids today will have a friend and a voice in these stories as they navigate a filter-, filler-, trolling- and perfection-filled world. I know I will. While there's enough and more discourse on body positivity online, there isn't one an Ozempic-fuelled reel or a shapewear advertisement won't interrupt. Even as someone who makes her living and name from social media, I must declare the cheap thrill the chosen format of *Hug Yourself* gives me. Thank god, this is a physical book. Kids, please read books. You can't scroll up and down, nobody tries to sell you things you don't need, and it's great for mental health.

A lot of the discourse on body image rests on the denial of it. The whole 'If you are not xyz, you are beautiful'. I have never understood why. It's almost as if someone speaking about their body—the way they feel and experience it—is too much of an inconvenience. Let's just call it beautiful and move on, because everything ultimately ought to be beautiful, no? (*cries in concealer and Facetune)

By not denying body image, *Hug Yourself* treats teenagers with the autonomy and respect growing adults deserve. It never talks down to them like their feelings right now are somehow invalid or non-serious because most of their life lessons are scheduled to happen later. It's exactly the kind of education and dialogue schools don't (or didn't in my time) provide and instead delegated to the 'real world'—a place almost everyone has a ticket to but refuses to pack for.

In the real world, I'm seen as someone who is body positive, radically accepting and almost celebratory of herself. In my inner world, I spend thousands every month to have my therapist remind me to be kind to myself, to remember I'm so much more than what I believe I lack. All this to dive back to Instagram and learn that I lack Korean glass skin, a Turkish rhinoplasty, a Brazilian butt lift, an Australian Koala, and god knows what else.

For me, *Hug Yourself* has begun to heal:

- the six-year-old Mallika whose mama gave her a 'boy cut', while other girls had long hair they put bows in;
- the eleven-year-old Mallika, who started to destroy her natural curls with heat because boys only liked girls with straight hair;

FOREWORD

- ♡ the thirteen-year-old Mallika whose boyfriend told her she had a 'beard';
- ♡ the eighteen-year-old Mallika, who was dumped for a skinnier girl, also named Mallika;
- ♡ the twenty-one-year-old Mallika, who lost half her hair to a traumatic life event and genetics;
- ♡ the twenty-four-year-old Mallika, who was convinced it was her perfectly tonged-and-sprayed salon curls and not her above-average copywriting skills that made her the boss's favourite;
- ♡ the twenty-six-year-old Mallika, who believed she was body positive and a total babe because the Internet said so one day;
- ♡ and the thirty-year-old Mallika, who believed she was an unattractive, ugly 'feminazzi' with a fat face and no trace of a neck because the Internet said so another day.

The Mallika today hopes to be a better friend to herself.

This book is for every teenager, parent, sibling, educator and guardian. Most importantly, this is for every troll, the most brutal of whom lives within us.

Mallika Dua
2024

EDITOR'S NOTE

Many years ago, I published a story called *When the Mountains Laughed*. It was about a dark-skinned boy who was convinced that he was so dark he could not be loved by anyone, ever. One day, the eight-year-old decided he could no longer bear the grief of being unloved and decided to climb a tall mountain and fling himself off it. It was a children's book, and my publishers asked me to edit the attempt at suicide part, which I did.

The story was about me—not the suicide part, just the despair.

I think I spent my entire childhood, adolescence and a part of my adult life convinced that I was unloved and unlovable because of my skin colour. Over the years, there have been several campaigns in India that have attempted to change the parameters measuring beauty. Thanks to such campaigns, we now have beautiful, dark-skinned

EDITOR'S NOTE

people in advertisements, on national television and walking ramps in fashion shows.

Besides what was happening around me, there were things that changed within me, too.

Somewhere in adulthood, I simply learnt to love myself and how I look. Now, no advertising or body shaming could create an emotional dent, ever. I also realized, how *that* shift was the only shift needed.

Once, I had a conversation with my very fair-skinned Sindhi sister-in-law, who was astounded to learn that I had suffered bullying and body shaming because of my skin colour. In her universe, skin-colour shaming does not exist. She, on the other hand, had been body-shamed for being flat-chested. It was a moment of epiphany. That day, I learnt that one kind of body-shaming awareness does not mean awareness of all kinds of bullying out there. The thing about shame is that we don't have the courage to talk about it.

Even with so much talk about body positivity today, body shaming is rampant in the digital world and cyber bullying, trolling and shaming have been fine-tuned into an art. Today, body shaming is still the easiest way to attack and wound.

We live in bubbles. Our universes are full of people we pick and choose. We tend to consume the kind of content that echoes our sensibilities, and, in many ways, in this era of super information, our lives have become more insular.

Just as my sister-in-law and I grew up believing there was only one kind of body shaming (ours), I believe that others also struggle with their own distinct body-image nightmares.

One day, two women and I got chatting about our experiences with our bodies. We had much to share. I told them about my conversation with my sister-in-law and how that dialogue had been revelatory. We agreed that in our entire lives, adolescence was the hardest, despite it being pre-Internet days. Was it possible that today's young struggle even harder than we did, not knowing all the possible stories of others struggling as well?

In the social media explosion that we live in, it is easy for all of us, especially our young, to forget that the reality portrayed in the digital domain is, in fact, fabricated. Photographs and videos are more about angles, lighting, poses and engineered situations of glamour. All the content spun is designed to keep you hooked, stay on the app and lure in more followers. But what it also does is fuel more self-doubt, more discontentment and more envy, while lowering confidence and creating unrealistic aspirations.

EDITOR'S NOTE

'Not a single book for adolescents on body positivity!' said Lakshmi Priya of Pachyderm Tales, one of the women in the conversation. We spoke about how distinct portrayals of teenagers in stories can impact readers' engagement in social comparisons and influence self-concepts. Studies show that merely knowing there are others out there who also struggle with the effects of body size (thin vs large) and body esteem (low vs high) has the power to lead readers to change their internal narrative, depending on how the stories end (sad vs happy).

We sighed, wishing there was more content for our young. Then we thought, *why don't we create that content?*

Hug Yourself has stories of triumph, resolve, resolution and a change in the way the protagonists perceive themselves. It has stories of skin (too dark, too fair, acne, disease), body size (too big, too small, too thin), stories where hair (hirsutism, alopecia, curly hair, premature greying) has been the bane of the protagonists' existence and a story where being good-looking was a challenge.

Can stories steer an adolescent away from negative thoughts and towards positive ones? Can a bunch of stories, so real, so visceral, make a reader relook at the way they perceive themselves? We certainly believe so. If nothing else, it is a collection of great stories by sixteen amazing authors who tell it like it is.

EDITOR'S NOTE

We hope that you read these stories and think. We hope the stories create space for dialogue and empathy. More than anything, we hope *Hug Yourself* is that book that will make you hug yourself every day and encourage conversations on body positivity that are real and empathetic.

Vinitha
2024

FIFTY SHADES OF GREY (HAIR)

Neha Singh

When I was a child, my mother used to slather my skin with a paste of haldi-besan-nimbu (turmeric-gram flour-lemon) to make it white and rub in *katoris* of warm coconut oil in my hair to make it thick, long and black. I guess there is a reason why everyone says I do the opposite of what the majority does. You see, as I grew older, my skin turned darker and my hair . . . white! No, not at twenty-five or thirty or thirty-five, but at fourteen!

The skin turning darker was definitely due to all the swimming I did in the scorching summer heat in north India. While other girls sat around the pool, sipping Thums Up and checking out boys in their swimming trunks, me and a few other *jhalli* girls were actually in the water, practising our underwater swimming techniques, playing water-dodgeball and swimming between the legs of friends without touching them.

Our skins got horrid tan lines that our mothers tried to scrape off with all kinds of home remedies: banana mashes, lemon juice, honey, curd, egg whites, turmeric, aloe vera . . . you name it. But that stubborn chlorine-water tan would refuse to go.

We were fine, because the tan meant we swam and that we were a group, a group of *us*. The fear of being the only one is so heightened when you are an adolescent. We were similar, and being in each other's company made us feel like the living example of the cliché: one for all and all for one, with the tan lines even creating the exact same 'skin-swimsuits' on our bodies.

I have no freaking idea how I got the grey hair, though. Chlorine? Maybe. Not putting enough oil in the scalp? Possibly. Medicare in the hair to get rid of lice? Probably. Genetics? Well, it could be. My mother, sister and father had jet-black hair, but my grandfather had a head of shocking white hair, and I remembered him like that ever since I could remember him at all.

The first white hair was easy to get rid of. I just popped the strand off my head and blew it out the bathroom window. *Gone with the wind,* I thought. But you know what they say about grey hair, right? You don't? Well, they say that never, never, NEVER pluck out a grey hair strand. Because, like a wild beast, it will come back with a vengeance that you will dread for the rest of your life.

As prophesied, it returned. The next week, I had three white strands, right in the hair parting. Well, two could play at this game of evil vengeance and destruction. *Pop! Pop! Pop!* I pulled out all three and set them free out of the window with a firm exhalation from my not-yet-toothpasted mouth. Done and dusted.

I suppose you can guess what happened the week after, and the week after that and the week after that. I lost. My evil white hair won. I had a tuft of white hair bang in the middle of my head now. Too bloody painful to pluck it all out.

It was time to seek out the healer of all ills, the saver of all lives, the knower of all tricks and the owner of all magic potions—my mother. Mummy.

Oddly enough, the woman who noticed everything, everywhere, at all times hadn't noticed the fact that I now looked like a mini-Indira Gandhi.

After letting out a short yelp, she got down to business like a surgeon who had conducted at least a thousand life-saving surgeries. Out came the magic ingredients from the witch's den—the kitchen. Henna powder, coffee powder, tea leaves, curry leaves, egg whites and dried hibiscus flowers. Yes! The cauldron was bubbling with the potion that was going to set everything right.

Except, it didn't! I now had a strange rust-burgundy-orange-brown tuft of hair right where the honourable whites stood a few hours ago. I think I spent days hoping that no one would address the rust-burgundy-orange-brown elephant in the room, and I think the others didn't really know what colour to call it, even if to just call it out! Thank god for small mercies, is all I can say.

A ritual was in place. Every two months, the iron *kadhai* would be brought out, and the henna paste with all the additives would be made. My head would then be masked in that I-can't-decide-whether-it-is-a-vomit-inducing-or-sweet-organic-smelling paste, and I would have it on for the whole evening. This meant, on that day, no friends would be entertained, no swimming would be done, no cycles would be raced, and no fun would be had, except watching some sad soap opera on the television. The next morning, I would sashay to school with my head smelling of henna and egg whites and my hair sporting that suspicious rust-burgundy-orange-brown ever-increasing tuft.

I am making it sound as if that's all I did during my teenage years. Of course not! I was winning debates, singing competitions and could swim fifty laps in the pool

FIFTY SHADES OF GREY (HAIR)

non-stop. But then, each time a boy I imagined having babies with in our small-but-charming wooden cottage in the Himalayas told me, 'I am not that into you,' I would blame my hair. Every heartbreak was neatly placed upon the fact that unlike other girls in town, I had freakin' white hair.

I would stare at myself in the bathroom mirror, tears trickling down my cheeks, asking god, 'Why me?' The swimming pool would be attacked with vengeance. I could now do seventy-five laps in one go—no one else could. I could dive from the highest diving board, the ten-metre one. In the swimming pool, I felt free of my hair. Thanks to the swimming cap! While other girls complained about the horrid rule of wearing ugly caps that made their heads look like boiled eggs, I was secretly thrilled that at least in the pool, I could stop obsessing about my white (well, technically rust-burgundy-orange-brown) hair.

I learnt several tricks to hide the white roots. I would put some kajal on the roots when they started showing. But this I had to stop when my first-ever boyfriend planted a kiss on top of my head (that was the only place allowed to him) and had black lips and nose after. Oops! Don't even get me started on what I said in my defense in that moment.

I started discovering new hairstyles and new partings of the hair that hid the whites almost perfectly. Except in sports class when we were playing volleyball or cricket, and I would forget all about the hair. The carefully done hair and the partings would turn rogue and punish me for having too much fun. Damn you, hair!

Even in those moments when I wanted to pull out my bestie's hair in a fight, I would resist, lest the fight led to the revelation of the nasty whites.

Each time a boy (or a girl) said to me with earnest eyes, 'I want to tell you something . . .' my heart would start pounding. *Oh god! Please, please don't tell me I have white hair. Coz, guess what? I already know,* is what I would think while saying my silent prayer. But strangely enough, except for Mummy and my sister, who routinely teased me about my whites, no one ever said anything about it. Maybe they were all blind. Or stupid, more likely.

My teenage years were well spent in the swimming pool, in the badminton court, in the ice-cream parlour and at the water cooler in school. All kinds of friendships were had, and all kinds of boyfriends were made.

Each date required pre-planning—henna and the whole paraphernalia. And then waiting a day extra for the smell to go away. No impromptu plans could be made. Of course not! The price of spontaneity would be too much to pay.

One day, while I had the horrid henna paste on my head and was sneezing because it was the dead of winter,

FIFTY SHADES OF GREY (HAIR)

my sister looked up from the fat novel she was reading and suggested the unthinkable.

'Why don't you just let your whites be?' she said with absolute nonchalance.

Have you ever had this feeling that your sibling has been put on this earth just to mess with your head and to irritate the hell out of you?

'Shut up and read your stupid book.'

I had stopped counting, but I now probably had a hundred whites on my head. I could also now swim a hundred laps in the pool, more than anyone else. Was I overcompensating for my hair? Or was the safe cover of the swimming cap making me spend longer hours in the pool? If only I had spent more time reflecting on my reasons for life choices at the time than worrying about my greys, I would have known the answer to that.

Time passed, and then one day, it was time to leave the town where I grew up.

Years passed. Older, wiser, more confident (can't say for sure, though), and now at a respectable enough age to actually have grey hair, I finally decided to listen to my sister and let my hair be. I stopped colouring my hair. The biggest, bravest decision of my life so far.

First, the roots started to show, followed by the strands and then the tufts.

'Hey, your hair looks nice!' a colleague would say. *Aah, she is just being polite.*

'The grey suits you,' a lover would say. *He just wants me to feel good.*

'You got so much grey. How old are you?' some not-so-sensitive friend would say.

But it didn't matter that much anymore. Not like it did in school. I was other things now. I was not the white in my hair. I was financially independent. I was a good, reliable and funny friend. I was a lover of stray animals and non-flowering wild plants. I was a great cook (Mother doesn't think so) who could stir up a nice meal for friends with leftovers within half an hour. I was a walker of unconventional paths and an ally of people on the edges of mainstream society. I was standing up for myself and for those who couldn't stand up for themselves. My life was full, and I wasn't painting my hair anymore. Instead, I was busy painting the town red with new-found adventures and a zeal to live to the maximum of my own potential.

But all these motivational-speech-type words came crashing down that horrid day when I was added to a WhatsApp group called School Reunion.

What? Why? God! Why me?! Just when everything was looking up.

To go or not to go was out of the question. The question that now hung in front of my eyes like a sharpened sword was to colour or not to colour.

Adolescent angst got the better of my adult confidence and wisdom and a L'Oréal non-ammonia deep brown colour was bought. The allergy test was done, and guess what? It turned out I was allergic to colour! Murphy's law is my least favourite law for a reason. Although I do thank god that I did the allergy test, but if I weren't allergic, forget the reunion, my school friends would have discovered my white hair only at my funeral.

Okay, maybe that's stretching it a bit too far. The reunion was just two days away. Not enough time to turn rust-burgundy-orange-brown. Should I just call in sick and not attend the reunion? No. Instead, I did the unthinkable. I went. Just like that.

Yes, you read that correctly. I wore my nicest dress with the nicest earrings, put on the nicest perfume and walked into that room.

Oh No! The guy who was supposed to be the father of my unborn babies in our small-but-charming wooden cottage in the Himalayas but was actually just not that into me, walked up and said, 'Hi! Aren't you the one who . . .'

Please, please, please don't say anything about my hair!

'. . . the one who swam a hundred laps? Bro, no one in the whole town could beat your record! You were just amazing!' he continued, his words pouring into my ears like honey.

I laughed, my pearly whites sparkling. (Not my hair, my teeth. You sure do have a one-track mind).

The reunion was fantastic. I met so many of my old friends. Some had white hair now, some didn't. Some had that strange colour I knew only too well. Others were definitely regularly using store-bought hair colour. Some of the boys (no, men) had receding hairlines now, while others were beyond saving. Some wore spectacles, some contact lenses. Some had put on weight. Some looked their age; some looked older, and some looked years younger.

But it didn't matter. We were all friends, meeting after ages but with the same warmth and openness with which we had accepted each other years ago. There were hardly any mentions of appearances and kilograms lost or kilograms gained. There were just long conversations about our mischiefs and our games and our loves and our friendships. We remembered the teachers that had taught us, the books we had read and discussed, the movies, the crushes and the adventures. We were proud of each other for what we had accomplished as individuals in our personal as well as professional and family lives. We were in awe of the ones who were walking on untrodden paths.

Late into the night, we were talking about the countries we had travelled to, the mountains we had climbed, the deserts we had crossed, the cultures we had experienced, the skies we had flown in, and the oceans we had swum in.

'You were the best swimmer of us all,' someone said, pointing at me.

'Hundred laps, right?' another chimed in.

'I am teaching my daughter how to swim, and I tell her, "You know there was a girl in my class who could swim a hundred laps without a break!"'

'The girl who swims a hundred laps. That's what even I remember you as,' a friend smiled.

'Me too!' another said.

How utterly strange. While I remembered myself as the girl with white hair, my friends remembered me as the girl who swam a hundred laps. My heart was so full that night.

Now, each day I look in the mirror and say, 'Hello, you! The girl who swam a hundred laps.' Because that's who I was. Just that I didn't know it then. But now I do.

FATTY BATTY AND THE FAT DEMONS

Anuja Chandramouli

I figured that staring at my face in a mirror was an exercise in extreme masochism. It always seemed to me like the damn thing was a gasp-of-horror-inducing, pock-marked landscape where there was irrefutable evidence of every skin ailment and facial imperfection known to be frowned upon in this supercilious world of ours. Since, by my own reckoning, I wasn't completely alienated from reason, I could also acknowledge that there was no need for such self-loathing. My face was actually fine and not really lacking in prettiness. While it was unlikely I would ever win a beauty pageant on its merits, my visage received more than its fair share of compliments which meant I was not quite as hideous as I imagined.

Unfortunately, this sliver of self-conscious awareness was not sufficient to allay the ever-present insecurity, which on particularly dark days made me want to rip my face off and offer it up as a burnt sacrifice to summon the Devil (Our English assignment is on Faust) so that I could sell my soul in exchange for the perfect countenance that would launch not a thousand ships (My essay on Helen of Troy won third prize at an inter-school competition) but at least a hundred blockbuster films. And commercials. Mercifully, I have not acted on my rash impulses. Yet. Besides, like God, I have a feeling the Devil doesn't bother to show up at your convenience. Damn them both!

Still, as excruciating an endeavour as it is to fixate on my face, it is a billion times worse when I turn my hypercritical gaze upon my naked body in a full-length mirror and take in the jiggly belly, which comes with a set of tyres and a spare, chunky thighs and flabby arms. As for my gargantuan behind (which will never command the adulation heaped on Kim Kardashian's generously proportioned derriere), I get through life pretending I don't have one. Forget gasping in horror; this painful moment of folly always induces a full-blown panic attack, which requires the exertion of every ounce of self-control I possess to stop myself from running like one possessed, screaming at the top of my lungs, and tearing out entire fistfuls of my hair! (My hair . . . don't even get me started.) In fact, the only thing stopping me from taking off in the aforementioned manner is the realization that this is India, and if I don't get arrested for indecent exposure or lewd and lascivious conduct, I would be stoned to death in the name of honour.

In case you haven't figured it out already, I have issues. And a far-from-healthy self-image. I always tell myself that these fixations are not quite debilitating. My parents may have thought differently, if they weren't otherwise engaged, but it is hard to say. They are not bad when they show up to check on their only child, but by my reckoning, parenting bores them to tears. Which doesn't bother me in the least because it is fun to be left to your own devices. It builds character.

Appa always says somewhat distractedly that I am perfect just the way I am and is enough of a lame dad to maybe mean it. Amma, who takes pride in the hourglass body she was born with and maintains without too much effort on her part, worries about my rotund shape and is forever consulting nutritionists and signing me up for stupid Zumba or CrossFit classes when she is not buying me exercise gear. But she usually has too much on her plate and does not have the time to follow up on her half-hearted intention to whip me into shape. Mostly, she contents herself with lecturing me about the evils of ordering junk on Swiggy and being less than religious about working out, then feels so bad for body shaming her flesh and blood that she surprises me with ice-cream cake, just in case I grow up to become a stripper and make her look like a lousy parent in the process.

It is a good thing I am adept at handling my problems. Regarding the appearance and weight issues, be they real or imagined, I deal with them (during, before and after school hours) by working out sporadically at the lousy classes Amma wastes money on and alternately starving myself and then eating my way through tubs of ice cream, drowned in hot fudge sauce, with a side of whipped cream and a bucket of chicken wings. If that doesn't make me feel better, I double down with mutton biriyani, onion raita and chocolate cake. Then, sick with self-loathing, I Swiggy in some sugar-free gelato to keep myself from feeling too horrendous about all the bingeing. If this doesn't stop the fat demons in their tracks, I don't know what will.

As for the relentless anxiety about stepping outside and allowing the world to scrutinize my grotesquely fat body and inevitable depression, I have it well under control. The trick is to keep busy. When not sleeping through classes in school as unobtrusively as possible, I spend most of my time cooped up in the bedroom, hunched over my homework, chatting with my friends online and watching whatever the adults aren't watching on Netflix, which is not the worst way to kill time. I am also working on developing mad skills. Amma insisted on making me join a Bharatanatyam class, which I attend as enthusiastically as the aerobics class she had paid for. I am also learning Japanese online, so I am not completely hopeless. But being indoors so much has made me pale and waxy like a vampire, which is better than venturing outdoors and risk being lynched by a fat phobic, frothing-at-the-mouth mob on the off chance that people see the morbidly obese monster I always see peeking out at me from the mirror.

Don't get the wrong idea. I am a long way off from requiring the attention of a shrink. Or padded cells. Or restraints. I go out once in a blue moon to take a break from neflixing and watch a movie starring Vijay Sethupathi or Shahid Kapoor. Or have pizza and milkshakes with my school friends who are not like those infamous mean girls on TV shows who fat-shame the poor unfortunates who don't have washboard abs. In fact, most folks in my life are understanding, even the well-meaning aunts who say that it is nice to finally see a 'healthy-looking' girl with child-bearing hips.

The only person who seems to have a problem with my body is me. But there is no helping that. Or my social life. Although I have been in a long-term relationship. It is with my dentist—necessitated by my sugar habit—and it is strictly professional, if excruciatingly painful for me, and sometimes for him as well. I have been known to bite.

My brief, exciting forays into the outside world notwithstanding, I mostly tend to remain in my room for months on end when not attending school. In here I stay and do my best to pretend that I am invisible. Sometimes, even with my friends. It is nobody's fault. I just can't help but think that since everybody is skinny and gorgeous, I am the only Fatty Batty at the party who might be attacked for the crime of corpulence at any given moment, with pitchforks and flaming torches.

My buddies are sympathetic if impatient with my chronic neurosis and bizarre fixation with the notorious fat demons. Worse, they always manage to look like they have stepped out of the pages of a fashion magazine. Next to them, I always feel shorter, fatter, frumpier and dumpier than I actually am.

The fact that everybody, including the optimal-weight challenged who seem to carry the excess fat deposits comfortably, makes me feel bad about myself is not a big deal. Everybody is insecure. Apparently, even superstars, who appear to have all the good things the world has to offer, served to them on a platter, are in a committed relationship with the head doctors who keep them plied with a steady supply of happy pills to fend off anxiety, panic, depression and suicidal impulses. It is strangely comforting to know that everybody is in the same boat and as miserable as can be. So, I am neither better nor worse than anybody else out there, barring the criminally insane who decapitate puppies and do other unspeakable things. And I would totally seek out therapy if I felt it were necessary. Or felt overwhelmed by the urge to do abominable things.

You probably wouldn't believe it, but I have never had a boyfriend. I know what you are thinking—what is the fifteen-year-old kid going on about boyfriends or their lack thereof! But to the aunty jis out there, none of us are as innocent as you unreasonably want us to be! All my friends, in fact, almost everyone in my section has a boyfriend or girlfriend. It is true! Iykyk.

My body-image issues are only partly to blame for the boyfriend situation. I am so certain they will hate my chubbiness and reject me that I make it a point to be prickly and completely unapproachable. But thanks to the global pandemic that arrived and hung around stubbornly with the gravitas of inevitable doom, my life took a momentary turn and, to my disbelief, sucked less.

The lockdown ensured that we were all cooped up like broiler chickens at home—scared, bored and haunted by the prospect of impending doom. Appa worked from home the entire day and most of the night. Amma had lost her job and took up baking in a ferocious bid to overpower the pandemic with positivity. Her surprisingly decent culinary efforts did not do my already-burgeoning waistline any favours. Damn her!

All of this would have been insupportable if not for the good offices of a much-reviled object, which, like Thanos, is inevitable. Of course, I am referring to our smartphones and assorted handheld gadgets which we possess and have unofficially sworn to have and to hold, for better or for worse, for richer or for poorer, in sickness and in health, to love, cherish and to obey, till death do us part . . .

Say what you want about the evils of gizmo addiction, but I was grateful for my tenuous lifeline to the outside world, which had filled me with so much anxiety in the past. It was nice to form connections in the digital space that were every bit as meaningful and fulfilling as the ones that I have kind of, sort of, somewhat negligently nurtured in the real world. For somewhere, in the murky depths of the matrix, I 'met' a dude. A real dude. Not one of those avatars or bots. He had the gentlest eyes you would have ever seen, and the thought of them still makes me feel all gooey inside, like the centre of a truly decadent caramel brownie. And no, you cynical thing, you! I was not being catfished. He does video reviews of the latest gizmos that have dropped on the market for a news media company on their YouTube channel.

I can't stress this enough, but he is a real person with flesh and blood and feelings and the rest of it. I had done my due diligence, and it is a good thing that privacy is dead in the surveillance state we live in today. Thanks to some snarky feedback I left on their website, we showed up on each other's radar, and by what feels like a miraculous happenstance, we were WhatsApping each other nonstop. I knew he was an older guy, but it was not a red flag because he was no creep. And he was so much smarter and fun to talk to than the boys my age, who are yet to grow out of their caveman personas and their excessive fondness for X-rated, adults-only content featuring but not limited to full-frontal nudity.

For the first time in my life, I found myself running around with a ridiculous smile plastered across my face. The funniest thing is that he seemed to think I was really beautiful . . . and smart . . . and funny! He texted as much, and every word and emoji oozed sincerity. Isn't that something? And isn't it nice when there is someone in your life with whom you feel really connected? With whom you can share all the stuff you dare not share with others? Who makes you feel special and interesting and awesome? He was, without doubt, the best thing that ever happened to me.

Unlike most of the guys out there, I don't think he was nice to me because he was hoping to make out with me and brag about it or something yucky like that. That is not to say we weren't being naughty and sharing forbidden fantasies, which is truly the stuff of modern romance.

We spent days and nights talking about everything and nothing. Have I mentioned that his voice is so mellow yet gravelly that it never failed to make me woozy and knock-kneed? Then I would replay the conversations we had over and over and over in my head till I was giddy with the awesomeness of true love. And dare I say it even though it is cringe? I was as happy as can be!

Things were chugging along perfectly, and I was basking in a radiance of pure contentment when it suddenly escalated. He wanted pics. Naked pics of the body which has been the bane of my entire existence. That made me hit the brakes hard. Do I? Do I not? Should I get indignant? It's not like tenth graders are not doing the sexting thing. They are. Cue loud gasps of horror, but it is true! So, even though I went silent on text, it needs to be said that I did try to do the needful. I clicked a billion pics from every flattering angle I could think of, aided by Internet tutorials and soft lighting, doing my best imitation of Barbie Ferreira.

In fact, I spent almost every hour of every day trying to produce nudes that were tasteful as well as raunchy. But it was all in vain. In my eyes, I still looked like one of those beached whales that show up on social media feeds of activists that go viral every once in a while, with the contents of their engorged bellies, which mostly consist of all the plastic and trash we dump carelessly into the oceans, displayed for our viewing pleasure. Clearly, the efforts of the eco-warriors were as fruitful as mine. With every buck of saved pocket money, I bought lingerie that cost a gazillion bucks per square inch. It did little to make me look remotely close to hot, let alone mouth-watering.

It dawned on me that the pics of me looking the way I did might accidentally drop on the Internet and go viral. A thousand memes would be launched. I would be expelled! Amma and Appa won't kill me, but they will be so sad and shamed in the eyes of the spiteful society we live in that I would want to kill myself. In a blind panic, I deleted everything.

Having given up on my pathetic attempt to be a topless model and quit while there were still a few shreds of dignity left, I coyly demurred to the love of my life despite his persistence. To my horror, the bugger started ghosting me, though I had been led to believe that we had something special. How could an unwillingness to keep the object of your affection plied with nudes end like this? Like all those before me who loved truly and intensely in the entire history of love and had their hearts smashed to smithereens for their efforts, I went bonkers. And by bonkers, I mean legit nuts.

Things got so hopelessly ugly that I was actually worried about myself. I wallowed. In grief and a surfeit of sugar and deep-fried food that Amma was whipping up in a manic, positive pixie frenzy in her quest to become a MasterChef. It must be confessed that I was so pathetically miserable that I even started casting white-magic spells thrown up by Google to steal his heart and lock it away within my own. To my surprise, it didn't work out. Neither did the Kamadeva mantra, which, according to YouTube, would fix my love life if I chanted it 108 times while staring at his photo. Then I bawled some more while contemplating sending him images of Bella Knox with my face morphed over hers before actually doing so. He sent me a smiley emoji and a heart. That was it. The next 5,000 messages I sent went unanswered. I lost my mind! More and more of it with every breathless second that stretched on unto infinity while I waited in vain for him to respond.

I stalked him relentlessly across social media. For days on end, I would force myself not to reach out to him before giving up and peppering him with messages that were supposed to be cool, breezy and witty, but which even I knew were desperate, pathetic and embarrassingly thirsty. Most were ignored, but he would respond with an emoji or a monosyllabic response once in a while, and suddenly, he would be my sun, moon and stars all over again. Then he would ghost me again, and I would be devastated. My grades slipped and then dropped badly. Again . . . and again. This went on and on and on.

Just when things couldn't get worse, they did. My phone fell into the potty and died. A part of me died, too. After I had spent the rest of the day trying to resuscitate the dead, I gave up and mourned the loss of my faithful companion, who had saved me from my loneliness and myself many a time. RIP, dear friend. We shall meet on the other side of the rainbow bridge where expired gadgets, that aren't lodged in the gullet of a hapless whale, wind up.

In retrospect, the loss of my phone wasn't the worst thing ever, although, initially, I was furious with my parents, who refused to replace it immediately. They felt my smartphone addiction was getting out of hand and insisted that my carelessness in losing it the way I had would do me a world of good. After I got over the impulse to scream at them for being tyrannical and all-knowing, I realized they were right. I needed to break up with the wonders of being constantly plugged into the Internet and take some time for myself.

To my surprise, I could be wise when the occasion called for it.

The digital space and its temptations relaxed their hold on me. I started reading again. And to my gratification, all the characters were as messed up as I was. I started studying and working on those flagging grades. Amma asked me to join a yoga class because Bharathanatyam/ aerobics/ Zumba and I had broken up for good. To her surprise, I agreed without kicking up a fuss. Believe it or faint, I enjoyed it and went regularly. Not because I was hoping to finally win myself an enviable body, but because it felt good to feel connected to my insides. It led to my not treating my physique like an enemy that needed to be bullied into submission.

After tuitions, instead of hopping into an auto, I walked back home. It felt nice to see life stirring again in a post-Covid world. Strangers smiled or waved at me, and I responded in kind. Sometimes, I would stop for some milky, sugary tea, and it tasted amazing. The samosa vendor *anna* always insisted I have an extra one for free, and I always accepted his kind offer. We even chatted if he was not too busy, and he promised to share his recipes for making the best deep-fried snacks in the world.

The mirror and I were still not getting along, but I didn't mind as much. I started going with Amma to volunteer at a cloud kitchen where meals were being catered for those afflicted with Covid, medical practitioners, health care personnel and social workers. Sometimes, we drove around with the leftovers and handed out nutritious meals to the poor, needy and hopeless, who thronged the streets in never-ending waves. They accepted the food with so much eagerness that it tugged at my broken heart. I didn't transform into Mother Teresa or anything, but at least I got a much-needed sense of perspective, which was almost as good.

To my pleasant surprise, I no longer felt like a hopeless case that was not deserving of love. That is not to say I stopped feeling 'fugly' and repulsive entirely, but I was easing into my own skin, and it felt like liberation and emancipation were not entirely beyond my reach. That was enough for me.

I still obsess over my ill-fated romance on certain dark days. My biggest worry is that all it would take is one lousy text from him, and I would fall back in love and spend every moment of every day sending him all the naked pics he wants. Ordinarily, the very thought of this happening (or not happening) would be enough to make me collapse into a hysterical bundle of nerves, but thanks to meditation and breathing exercises, I am managing. The good news is that I don't think about him all the time. Mostly, the focus is on myself. And occasionally, the very hot Jacob Elordi.

School is going to start soon, and the boys there are as hopeless as ever, but maybe there will be some new students . . . Who knows? Perhaps I'll find someone who speaks the same language as me. Wouldn't that be nice? But even if I don't meet anyone in the immediate future, I am going to shrug it off. It isn't the end of the world, after all. I could be wrong about that, too. And that is perfectly alright.

If Covid has taught us anything, it is that the apocalypse can sneak up on you when you least expect it to, but that's fine. I no longer hate myself or my body, and I plan to head out and meet my annihilation armed with a tub of dulce de leche as well as the bits and pieces of self-esteem I have patched up together. That is the best I can do for myself, and it is not the worst way to live . . . or die . . . or so I like to think. And I am probably right. Wouldn't you agree?

HILLS AND VALLEYS OF NANGELI

Vidya Nesarikar

'Amma, do you know the story of Nangeli?'
'You mean the woman from Kerala who cut off her breasts? Yes, I have heard about her. She did it as a mark of protest,' said Amma, knotting her eyebrows in a frown.

'Well, I want to cut mine off. I, too, want to protest,' said Dharti.

Amma was used to her fiery child and her outbursts. When she was in this mood, it was best to go along with her.

'You do know she bled to death after she cut off her breast, don't you?' asked Amma.

'Inconsequential consequence,' shrugged Dharti.

'Well, forgive me, but I would like you alive and fighting for your causes, if that's okay. And as your amma, I do hope I have some say in this. So, no more talk of cutting off breasts.'

They were sitting there, mother and daughter, one in front of the other. Amma was putting oil in Dharti's hair. It was their happy time. Amma parted the hair and used her fingers to put warm drops of fragrant coconut oil on the pale scalp.

'Why this sudden urge anyway?' Amma asked after a pause. 'What are we protesting?'

'Amma, I hate my large breasts. I wish I was flat-chested,' Dharti said dejectedly.

'*Kanna*, breasts nurture life. They are the mammary glands. And just like noses or feet, they come in all sizes.'

'I wish they grew only when they were needed. What nurturing of life should I do at fifteen? I barely manage to nurture myself. Also . . . this may be a good time to tell you that I killed the money plant,' she added sheepishly.

'Again?' Amma said in mock disbelief.

'Well, back to the topic. I wish they were detachable!'

'Haha! Now there's a thought . . . Oh! Or deflatable!' Amma said and giggled.

It was Dharti's turn to laugh.

'But Amma, seriously, why does the school uniform have a dupatta only for girls? We are supposed to hide them and pretend they don't exist. But everyone knows they exist.'

'Yes, they do. The hills and valleys—that's what we called them when I was your age.'

'Amma, do you know there are over one hundred nicknames for breasts? Who comes up with these? Who has all this time?!'

'Oh, believe me, people have a lot of time for nonsensical activities,' sighed Amma.

'Breasts are sexualized for no fault of theirs—especially big breasts. The judgements passed. The unnecessary comments. The unwanted attention received. What is one to do? I want a T-shirt that says, "NOTHING TO SEE HERE, JUST BREASTS".'

'Order two T-shirts, *kanna*.'

But this time, Dharti ignored her amma's joke. 'I hate that so many girls wear a sweater over their uniforms. Many girls have dropped out of sports because they don't want to run on the field. Some slouch, while others try and hide under an umbrella when walking back home,' said Dharti. She was trying hard to hold back her tears. 'Whatever you wear, it's always *your* fault. Whatever happens, it is always *your* fault. So, what's the point of a dupatta?' Dharti said, ending her speech with a sigh.

Amma looked on quietly.

'You know, a friend of mine said her dream was a simple one,' continued Dharti, 'to run at a zebra crossing—wild and free—without worrying about all the people in their vehicles with their headlights on, staring at her chest.'

Amma's eyes welled up. She wished she could soothe her daughter. She wasn't as articulate as her, but she understood her pain all too well. After all, these very thoughts had crossed her mind, too, as a teenager. Only she had just accepted it as the way things were.

Don't wear this . . . Don't wear that . . . Where is your dupatta . . .? Isn't that neckline too deep . . .? Aren't you too fat for that dress . . .? Do you know beauty queens have a 36-26-36 frame . . .? Why don't you go on a diet . . .? Why are you wearing something so tight . . .? This won't fit you . . . Go to a tailor . . . Get something loose stitched . . . Whose attention do you seek? Learn to keep a low profile . . . Lower your gaze . . . Keep your head down . . . Don't talk back . . . You are here to study . . . What will people say . . .? This is not a fashion show; this is life . . . You have to live in this society.

The words echoed in her head. She felt fifteen all over again. The anxiety resurfaced.

But here was her daughter, protesting like Nangeli against the unfair breast tax. A bizarre tax in the nineteenth-century kingdom of Travancore that had to be paid by women of the supposed lower castes if they wanted to cover their chest. Was covering the chest a privilege reserved only for upper-caste women? Couldn't women choose what they wore and what they wanted to cover or not cover? Did the male gaze have to decide their dress code?

Whether it was covering up or not covering up, both were two sides of the same coin. *How much had actually changed from then to now?* she wondered, looking at her daughter.

'You keep your head held up high and your spine upright, *kanna*. Nangeli may have had to resort to extreme methods because such were the times, but you have a mightier weapon.'

'What's that, Amma?'

'Your words.'

'But what should I write about, Amma? How does one start a change?'

'By making a start,' Amma said simply.

And then, Dharti picked up her pen and began to write:

♡♥

Am I breasts attached to a body?
    Or a body attached to breasts?

Don't you see?
The red earth is in me.
Hills and valleys, oceans and rivers,
Cracks and crevices,
A deep, dark pit you only pretend to understand.
Tear them off.
Bleed to death.
But you still fail to see.
You dig, plunder, extract and loot.
You corner me, point fingers at me.
Say fault lines lead to catastrophe.
Can the ocean be contained?
This is my body.
My proud chest
Nurturing life.
Spit and blood and sweat.
Skin that tastes of salt.
Scars and folds.
The way the river bends.
You ask me to conform.
I will not.
I will not.
I will not.

SECOND SKIN

Vibha Batra

It's Saturday evening, and I'm working on an assignment. How exciting! But hey, it's due on Monday, and all I have so far is the title.

My fingers fly over the keyboard. I type-delete-repeat.

I'll probably go with option 1: Spending time with my family. You know, eventually. Like all my classmates. Option 1 checks all the boxes: plausible (if not entirely true); acceptable; feel-good; fail-safe. For now, though, it's option 2 that's taking up all my headspace.

Covid Cloud, Silver Lining

by

Meher Basheer

Masks. The one good thing that came out of the pandemic. Forever masker, oh yes, that's me.

> The truth is, I've been hiding since forever. Behind sunglasses, caps and dupattas. Still, behind a mask is when I feel truly free. The only time I feel the same as everyone else. The only time I get treated the same as everyone else. The only time they—'well-intentioned' relatives, frenemies, complete strangers—don't bring up my looks. Or rather, the lack of them. Behind a mask, I forget about my cleft lip and palate . . .

I'm so busy typing that I don't hear the knock.

'Hey,' Mom pokes her head into the room. 'For someone who hates their room, she sure spends a lot of time in there,' she speaks over her shoulder.

I look up from my laptop, half-turning in my swivel chair.

'Meher Basheer,' she says, placing her hands on her hips. 'Is this your idea of limiting your screen time?'

'Working on my assignment, Mo—,' I say as she throws the door open.

The word lodges in my throat as someone walks in.

It's him! Aarav. He's been in my head, in my nightmares. And now, he's in my room. Again.

Panic floods my body. A cold sensation grips my stomach. Goosebumps erupt on my arms.

'. . . spends all her waking hours on her phone. When she's not video chatting with Delnaz, she's watching videos . . .' Mom rambles on, blithely unaware of the effect Aarav's presence has on me. '. . . and don't even get me started on social media. Her grades have been slipping. Tonnes of complaints at the PTM; don't even ask . . .'

As she offloads, I spring to my feet. Strategically stepping behind my chair, shrivelling behind the barrier, shrinking into myself. *What's he doing here?* I rail at Mom silently.

'Del's dropping by,' she had said, completely neglecting to mention Aarav was coming, too. Had I known, I'd have made a plan or some random excuse and totally bailed.

Our parents, they meet all the time. The Kapoors, the Sethnas and the Basheers have been friends for ages. Back in the day, they used to drag us to all the get-togethers.

Sounds crazy now, but Aarav, Delnaz and I were inseparable. But that was before. Before he shot up and morphed into the school hottie and amassed quite a fan following. Before he discovered he had amassed quite a fan following. Before he realized he didn't want to hang out with two losers. Yup, friendships have a before and an after, too. Quite like those fairness (brightness?) cream and weight-loss advertisements. Thankfully, it was around this time that our folks stopped forcing us to tag along.

'. . . Why can't you be like Aarav?' Mom's voice cuts into the flashback. 'Such a good boy. A straight-A student, star athlete . . .'

School sicko, I seethe silently.

'You're too kind, my lady,' he doffs an imaginary hat, bowling Mom over with his (barf!) grace and charm.

'High time Meher got serious about her studies. Tell her na, beta.'

Aarav turns the full force of his reptilian gaze on me. Aarghhh! Where's a mask when you need one?

Unbelievable. He can actually look me in the eye. After everything that transpired. And that confidence has nothing to do with looks . . . Yeah, right! Here I am, sick with nerves and overwhelmed by nausea. Not for the first time, I long to be someone else. Like those bright-happy-shiny folk who stare down at us from hoardings, sashay down ramps, star in blockbusters and advertisement campaigns alike and grace the covers of glossy magazines. Like those normal-regular-average fifteen-year-olds who post their selfies on their socials. What wouldn't I give for that superpower?

'I'll see what I can do, Aunty.' Aarav's back is towards her when he talks, so she can't see the creepy smirk on his face.

My skin crawls. Bile rises to my throat. How did I ever think his smile was cute? That *he* was cute? And gorgeous and hot and awesome and all those things everyone thinks he is?

Mom flashes him a grateful smile. She turns around to leave, but not before making sure the door is held open by the doorstopper. It's about the only helpful thing she's done.

'W-w-wait,' I say, pushing the chair away and hurrying after her, 'I'll help you set the table.'

Mom swivels me around like the aforementioned piece of furniture. 'I'm sure you kids have lots to catch up on. Delnaz is on her way. Will send her upstairs. I am swiggying pizza, okay?'

Then Mom's gone and I'm alone in the room with Aarav. Just like that evening.

'Del's on a diet,' I call out from the doorway, my voice shrill.

'Isn't she always?' sniggers Aarav.

The tune of 'Characteristically Cruel' plays in my head. I whirl around to tell him off, but the words get lodged in my throat again. My guitar—scratch that—my *life* is in his hands.

He idly plucks at the strings, looking up to wink at me. Anyone who knows me would tell you it's my sanctuary, the one good thing in my life. My fingers tighten around the doorknob. I know what he's doing. He's trying to mess with my head . . . and succeeding.

Should I snatch it out of his hands and risk making contact? Stay rooted to the spot and watch as he toys with my life? I'm saved the trouble of making a decision because he casts the guitar aside, bored already.

As he looks around the room, I wonder if he remembers. If he remembers every little detail of that evening the way I do. If he regrets and repents. If he ever plans to apologize and beg for forgiveness.

No such luck. He plonks down on my bed, patting the spot next to him.

'Stop!' I burst out. 'Just stop it!'

'Or what?' he challenges, his eyes gleaming with malice. 'What you gonna do?'

The knot of tension in my stomach starts to make its way up.

'Or I'll tell everyone what you did.' My voice is feeble and shaky. The threat hollow, like my guitar when it's not properly connected to the amplifier, even to my own ears. He knows I'll do no such thing. He always knew he'd get away with it. He was counting on my silence. Still is.

'What did I do?' he asks innocently, as if nothing happened. As if he didn't grab me. As if he didn't try to kiss me, even though I'd made it perfectly clear it wasn't something I wanted. As if he didn't call me names for resisting his advances. In this very room. Not too long ago.

He doesn't wait for me to answer. 'Think they'll believe it?'

I couldn't believe it either. You know, when he first texted me. Someone like him into someone like me. In what parallel universe? The coolest person on campus was flirting with me when he could have had his pick of the school's hottest girls. How could he possibly be interested in me? Me, of all people. The only kind of attention I had ever received was negative. Precisely why I told no one. Not even Del. And we've been BFFs way before the term was invented. Precisely why I refused to take it seriously. Precisely why I shut him down.

God! He was persistent. And charming. And sweet. Not just online. IRL too. I remember it like it was yesterday. It was right after I'd made that disastrous presentation. Stumbling, stammering, stuttering my way through the slides, punctuating the entire thing with apologies. It was tragic. Right up there on the most-embarrassing-moments-ever list. When the agonizing class finally, *finally*, drew to a close, Aarav did something he'd never done in school: he acknowledged my existence. 'Nailed it,' he smirked, brushing past me on the way out.

I mean, I'm only human. I started texting him back, allowing myself (rather foolishly, I must add) to feel different. Not as ugly as they said, or merely an object of pity or ridicule. Not something to gape at or whisper about.

Not just a scar-and-sob story. But something more. Almost normal. Okay, normal adjacent. Normal adjacent(ish).

It's why I had agreed to let him come over. That evening when our parents were out, grabbing dinner and catching a late-night movie. It's why I had let him come up into my room. To talk to him. To get to know the cooler/hotter/popular version of my dorky childhood friend. And, yeah, to hang with my latest crush. Turned out, talking was the last thing on his mind.

'My word against yours, Scarface,' he drawls, pausing the flashback. It was like a punch to the gut. You'd think it would hurt less having been called that all your life. Tears prick behind my eyes. It gets to me. Every. Single. Time. Well, here's the thing. If you grow up listening to that stuff, you start to believe it, you internalize it. It becomes a part of you, your second skin. A constant companion, along with shame and guilt and self-loathing.

He pushes himself off the bed, drawing himself to his full height. Taking over the room, dwarfing everything around, especially me. He stalks up to my desk. My eyes fly to my current read. It's an easy prey: open, upside down.

I abandon my post and step away from the door. Too late. He swoops down on the books. 'Love Yourself: The Loser's Guide to Self-Acceptance,' he reads out loud with a mock-serious expression. 'So, do you?'

Love myself? Let's see. How could I possibly love myself when every single message I receive—from my family, the society, the media, the whole world—tells me I'm not worthy . . . of love, affection and respect. How could I possibly love myself when my parents don't? Multiple surgeries, a rhinoplasty, endless hospital visits and countless heartbreaks later, Mom still insists on dragging me to doctors, healers and soothsayers. And Dad . . . he does nothing to stop her.

'Sorry, sorry, sorry about the hold-up!' Delnaz bursts into the room. Her eyes pop out of her skull as she spots Aarav.

'Chubster,' he sneers by way of greeting. 'Will leave you losers to it, then.' He sweeps out of the room. I slump against the wall.

'OMG! AK in the flesh! What's he doing here?' Delnaz squeals with excitement.

I've been wondering the same thing. Delnaz starts to say something, hesitates, then clams up. She seems to be struggling with a decision. That's new. 'Del, what's going on?'

She blushes a deep scarlet. 'I-I've been meaning to talk to you about something.'

I bob my head and make encouraging sounds.

'I don't know how to say this . . . you'll never believe this,' she says in a conspiratorial whisper. 'I mean, I keep pinching myself . . . but it's for real! Guess who has a crush on me?!'

There's a sinking feeling in the pit of my stomach. I have this awful feeling—a sense of impending doom. Please god, let it not be true.

A dreamy look comes over her face. 'I thought Aarav was pranking me!'

My heart stops. I can't breathe. All I hear is a roar in my ear that won't die down. She goes on, oblivious to the storm that rages in my heart.

'Sending all those flirty texts and DMs . . . making eye contact at school, of all places! You know, he smiled at me the other day, and I literally died!' She says with undisguised glee. 'It's *insane!* I mean . . . look at me,' she points to her plus-sized frame, 'and look at *him!*'

'You're perfect! You hear me?'

She goes on as if I haven't spoken. 'When was the last time you saw him at a get-together?' Her hands fly to her mouth. 'This can mean only one thing . . .'

'It doesn't mean a thing,' I snap, sounding more uncharitable than I'd intended to be.

A look of confusion comes over her face.

I get it, okay. She's on cloud nine, she's flying high. Her crush is into her. Or so she thinks. There's only one thing to do. Bring her down to terra firma with a thud.

'You're reading too much into it, Del.' I hate what my words do to her. Puncture her excitement. The happy gas leaves her. Her shoulders slump.

'You don't deserve him.'

She looks me in the eye. 'You mean, I'm not good enough for him. Why don't you say what you really want to?'

My heart breaks. Del. Del. Del. My beautiful, sweet, smart, kind Del, who, like me, equates a media-and-society-approved appearance with beautiful, who battles all the microaggressions that come with being a certain shape and size in this unfair world, who thinks she takes up too much space and is somehow less because of it.

I glance at my guitar, picture Aarav strumming the strings and that's when it hits me—I didn't choose the chords. All this time, I've been singing a tune that's not mine. Playing a song someone else composed, but no more. The music's going to be mine. It may not be perfect, and it may not be original—an inspired take at best. It may be unfamiliar and unsure, and I may even end up breaking a few strings, but it's going to be every bit worth it.

In that moment, it happens. I shed my second skin. Dropping the mask of shame, I break the seal of silence and rip through the layers of rejection that make me, ME. I stand up, reaching out to grab her wrist. 'Come on.'

'What? Now? Where?' I don't give Del time to react.

I take a deep breath and brace myself. 'There's something you should know; there's something *all* of you need to know . . .'

I trot down the stairs, unceremoniously tugging Del along.

Three pairs of grown-ups (and the rotten teen) playing cards at the dining table glance up in surprise.

'Pizza is in the kitchen,' Mom puts her cards down and starts to get to her feet.

'You'll want to sit down for this,' I say softly.

The FFFs (Family Friends Forever) look bewildered.

'What's going on?' asks Kapoor Aunty.

I tell her exactly what's going on. I tell them everything. I don't mince words. I don't hold back. '. . . And I don't know what Aarav's told you about his broken nose, but he sure didn't break it on the sports field,' I finish.

Once I am done, only then do I look at Aarav.

'Bullshit,' he scoffs. But the smile on his face is tight, his 'Fair-and-Lovely' skin is blanched, and that famous swag is conspicuous by its absence.

A deafening silence shrouds the room. Then, I burst into tears.

'You should leave,' Dad says in a hushed voice.

'. . . was about to,' I reply silently. But when my gaze travels to him, I find he's looking at the Kapoors.

'And don't bother coming back,' adds Mom. My eyes fly to her. And I know that it all makes sense to her now. The inexplicable revulsion towards my room, the sudden dip in my grades, the uncharacteristic behaviour, everything.

Chairs are pushed back. Voices are raised. Fingers are pointed. Barbs are traded. Insults are hurled. Words are exchanged—words I wouldn't repeat in polite company. The Kapoors, renowned in our circles for their colourful vocabulary, are in their element.

As the curtains go down on more than just the evening, Del turns to me and says wistfully, 'I wish *I* had headbutted AK.'

MS JASMINE JAW

Aditi De

The universe was in a foul mood that day. Moody. Broody. Flying chicken feathers rained on Adz out of a gulmohar tree, courtesy of an escapee from the school coop. The culprit showed little remorse but made absurd sounds among the boughs. It was neither English nor Mandarin nor Bangla. Did the global, artificial language Esperanto sound like that?

Adz felt as if she was in the eye of a storm. She cared little if the constructed international auxiliary language was mastered by teenagers or chickens. But a shower of stray feathers could not be a good omen. Through the gulmohar boughs, light streamed down on Adz. Red-faced, wild-haired, she pelted towards the hostel for a quick shower.

Months ago, Adz had confided her favourite dream in her bestie Sanaaya at their all-girls school. She wished to be a shower of light. Much like the comforting radiance she felt when her tall, handsome Baba kissed her forehead. But he had left the planet just months before. Drat that heart attack!

Adz now felt as if even flickering diyas cast shadows through her nights . . . and days. It mattered little what Reynolds Sir had taught them in the eighth grade: light casts no shadows because all emitted rays move away from the original source.

Her Libran mind could not wrap itself around recent reality bites. Within her buzzy brain, within her ultra-skinny, vertically challenged frame, Adz lacked the words to sum it all up. Cow poo? Gross? Life sucked. It just wasn't fair. In an all-capitals SCREAM.

Mentally, Adz cartwheeled back to that surreal day. To when her house captain Mira Jija (it, *jija*, is the Rajasthani word for didi or *akka*) stopped Adz and Sanaaya as they peacefully strolled towards their hostel in Jaipur after tea. Having accidentally watched Adz on the 400-metre track, Mira Jija insisted that she represent Florence Nightingale in the inter-house sports. Just because Adz was tinier than others her age.

Adz cringed, cried and then reluctantly agreed to join the field as a sub-junior athlete in the 100-metre sprint. How would that look when all her classmates at thirteen plus were either juniors or seniors on the track? At 1.3

MS JASMINE JAW

metres and lighter than thirty kilograms, Adz could not easily talk her way out of the impasse.

She had not figured out how to psyche her body into the lightness of being. Whenever she had played pretend-princess as a child, she did not evoke a floss-brained, blue-eyed, yes-saying blonde. Instead, she conjured up the beauteous, horse-riding, tennis-playing Maharani Gayatri Devi of Jaipur. Or the curvaceous, dusky Rihanna with her Coca-Cola voice. Or the lithe-limbed speed goddesses, like Kenyan marathoners Eliud Jepchirchir or Brigid Kosgei at the Tokyo 2020 Olympics. Adz sighed loud and long. Her awkward gait, her growing bust, her body seemed to belong to another.

After sessions on the track, Sanaaya learnt that her bestie needed more than a wrap-around hug to heal this time. Especially since her Baba was unreachable now. And her Ma did not quite help with her diktats. ('Don't sprawl; sit with your legs together' or 'Play more basketball to grow taller' or 'You are not a lawyer; stop being so argumentative.')

'But . . . but all the other sub-juniors will be way younger than me,' Adz had protested to Mira Jija, looking down at her sturdy black shoes.

'Shall we give it a try tomorrow?' Mira Jija had refused to relent. 'Meet me on the 400-metre track at 6.00 a.m., before the PE sessions begin.'

Adz pleaded with her eyes to be let off the hook. But the tall, willowy Mira Jija had other ideas—of trophies, of glory, of adding points to the Florence Nightingale house tally.

Adz cursed her own look, her luck and her frame. Was this her karma because she regularly poured the malai-topped eggnog with honey into potted plants around the hostel? They grew taller, stronger and glossier by the day. Her fingers touched the brown birthmark over the right salivary gland on her whiter-than-clouds face. The three-petalled jasmine-bloom shape sent *prana* pulsing through her fingertips. Baba had persuaded her that the signature petals were the sign of a winner. No matter if she wanted to be a writer, sprinter or a lawyer, like Amal Clooney. Or even a mother to a whole football team.

'On your marks, get set, go!' became the background score of all her waking moments in the three weeks leading up to Sports Day and often spilt over into her wilder dreams, but with one vital difference. In Adz's dreams, her body was the perfect hourglass. Like her fuller, taller classmates. Not like the Warli-style stick figures that she resembled in waking life. These freaking games felt like the Olympics to Adz. *Faster! Higher! Stronger!* Adz watched her classmates sprint through the 4 x 100-metres relay that breezy February morning as she tried to delete the feather shower from her mind. Tugging at their socks for luck, the participants' eyes squinted in the direction of the baton-bearer surging towards them. They took off in a flurry of movement, their pumping arms, thighs and toes synchronized to move in rhythm, and their breasts bobbing in time.

Envy permeated Adz like an invisible rash on a guinea pig, for within her white sports shirt, all she could spy were two tiny vanilla cupcakes, each topped with a largish raisin. Why couldn't she belong to this girl gang in bloom? The mutinous cupcakes remained silent. That did not help. Then, through her foggy mind, Adz heard the call for the 100-metre sprint for sub-juniors and took her position on the track. Sanaaya ran up, hugged her and whispered exactly what she needed to hear. Would their plot work?

There were eight lanes (with two lanes per house) representing the Sarojini Nadu, Helen Keller, Marie Curie and Florence Nightingale houses. The other seven keen-eyed younger sprinters limbered up. They stretched, they twisted, and they warmed up. So did Adz, her limbs moving of their own volition, like an automaton. The other sub-juniors smiled sheepishly at Adz, unsure of how to greet her or whether to wish her luck. Intuitively, she touched her indelible petals, a talisman she believed in.

A false start almost took its toll. Then they geared up to begin again, the crouched runners' fingers touching the track near their toes. Their eyes were trained on the finishing line. Spontaneously, Adz had chosen to run barefoot and tossed her canvas shoes aside.

The clapper sounded like thunder. They were off once again!

All Adz wanted was for the embarrassing sprint to end. Her mind silently chanted, *you can do this. Lose, Adz, lose.* Her eyes almost closed, her legs pumping like a peppermint-fuelled zombie, Adz inhaled the desert sun. She heard the thudding of feet on the parallel tracks.

Adz met the chalk line at 100 metres. Then she ran an extra twenty-five metres blind. She collapsed on the turf, hugging her knees. She prayed she would not barf. Tugging at the tufts of grass snagged between her toes, she closed her eyes.

Mira Jija, her eyebrows tinted with sand from the high jump pit, leant over Adz. 'You won,' she said, holding out her hand. 'Everyone else came in a few seconds after you.'

Ms Jasmine Jaw, Adz whispered to her primed, skinny body. *What's wrong with you?*

Her mind in overdrive (synced to a BTS song teeming with the cute-faced Korean boy band she was crushing on) asked: *Why, why, why should running be about winning and losing? Why couldn't she just run for joy?*

At the long-jump pit an hour later, the turbulence of bubbling jalebis in Adz's belly had turned to *murukkus*. Should she plead illness? Should she quit? *Lucky petals, don't let me down*, she pleaded. *I need to lose.*

Adz flexed her toes. She pulled her right knee to her chest and then her left one. She was aware that she was not the most athletic teen she knew. She obsessed over somersaulting, but her spine was as inflexible as an iron rod. As for *shirshasana* during yoga, her legs refused to rise to the occasion, while her arm-cushioned head flopped to the left or right. Even her bulkier classmates could do it, but not Adz.

She had no clue how the other sub-juniors had fared as she approached the long-jump pit. A left step and a right. Faster and faster till her right foot hit the take-off board. Her legs air-pedalled hard to gain inches and her blue-veined arms flapped mid-air. She landed hard on her back, almost collapsing. Ouch! That hurt. Two more tries, each more reluctant than the last. She steered herself away from the jumps registered on the officials' iPads.

Way too soon, Mira Jija ran up to Adz again. 'The second-best jump among the sub-juniors is yours,' she whispered.

Adz buried her face in her fists, invisibly pummelling back the waterfall of unshed tears. The sky and the grass seemed to swap places. She pleaded with the horizon to swallow her up. She strolled over to a gaggle of her eighth-grade classmates. Harbinder, Anisa, and even Neelam jumped with joy. But Sanaaya could read her tell-tale body language. The hesitant stride, the angled elbows, the unclenching and clenching of fists—her BFF knew that emotions raged within Adz, waiting to implode. Anger. Confusion. Belittlement. Warring identities.

When Adz slow sprinted to the awards platform to a crescendo of Florence-Nightingale applause, her face was mottled red. Her win in the sprint and her second place in the long jump added up to make her the best sub-junior athlete. But she felt like a scrambled Rubik's cube. Her sports triumph felt like a tragedy. Why had her imperfect body let her down? Why did it matter little to Mira Jija that tiny Adz was among the top three in her class academically? Or that she was feted as a budding poet by her parents and even her teachers? Or that she shone for Florence Nightingale at elocution, debates and theatre?

Adz buried the silver cup under her mattress in the dormitory and made a perfect bed over it. Taut sheets. Her blanket folded in a triangle (what else was geometry class for?).

'Adz,' sang Ahalya as she passed the newly minted sports champ rummaging through her messy cupboard. 'Can I have a look at your cup of joy?'

'I've kept it safely. Not sure where exactly.' Adz dodged her eyes. 'Later maybe?'

As Adz tossed about under her blanket that night, she heard her Baba's voice, soothing, calm and understanding. He patted the spot beside him, her favourite place, on the padauk divan in their sun-drenched living room. 'Don't be afraid to be yourself, Adz *shona*.' Baba's voice felt like a tender hug. 'Or to ask for help when you need it. You are unique. Remember, you were born to be a winner.'

Adz touched her lucky petals in her sleep. She sighed and smiled.

♡♥

By the time she was fifteen, Adz felt her body change. Her cupcakes had morphed into wannabe muffins while she perched on a better-cushioned derriere. Her face changed every day, even as Adz practised her pout in the hostel mirror, all to impress the dimpled Bangtan-boy, Jin, lookalike next door come summer break. But would he even look at Adz? Especially since her birthmark had spread to resemble a barely tattooed bloom. A bloom that could not be scrubbed off, no matter the coffee mask or the bleaches Adz experimented with.

The final year at school was a blur. Adz declined to be a Florence Nightingale prefect. She chose not to yell 'eyes right' or 'stand at ease' at a bunch of juniors, no matter how puppy-cute their eyes were. She picked the weirdest combination for her board finals: English literature, Spanish, history, chemistry, mathematics, visual arts, individuals and societies. She even excelled at her choices. All thanks to not burning the midnight oil. But mainly because she could escape to her 'Baba-zone' at will whenever the going got tough.

Her peers could not quite figure out her non-conformist personality, her bubbly mind and her quirky heart. She was *sick*. Or was she evil?

Just days before their board exams, an epic inter-school debate contest loomed on the horizon. It was about the state of the world and the rights and responsibilities of being a contemporary child. Minutes before standing at the lectern for Florence Nightingale, Adz did the *anulom-vilom* yogic breathing and took a few deep breaths. Then, departing from the practiced script, she darted into the unknown.

'Why do we need a world with borders and countries? Or passports and visas? Or minds that feel a swan-white skin like mine is superior to a yellow, brown or black skin? When I am an adult, I will write the stories of the voiceless, the oppressed, the Dalits, the slaves. No one else can live that dream for me . . .'

As she drew in another lungful of air, the guest judge looked puzzled, his chin cupped in his hand, his brow furrowed.

'Why don't our schools teach us that Indian, Pakistani, Chinese, Nepali, Bangladeshi and Sri Lankan children can be friends? I know I will easily make friends with teenagers like me across borders. Why don't our teachers and our parents give us a say in the world we want?'

The judges went into a huddle once the thirteen student speakers had said their pieces. Adjusting his lapel mike, the guest judge announced that the best speaker cup went to Adz. It was a unanimous verdict.

'Where did your radical thoughts come from?' he asked Adz, holding out his hand. 'You stood out as more confident, true to yourself . . .'

'I don't want only virtual friends,' Adz responded. 'Or to live only on social media information. I dream of a peaceful world. One that is not full of adult conflict or on the brink of a world war. If you deny us this wish, we, as children, will have to claim this birthright . . .'

He nodded and shook her hand once more.

As Zainab, Lara, Harbinder and Krittika walked Adz to the classroom, they stopped under the umbrella-spread of the neem tree to catch their breath.

'Look girls!' exclaimed Zainab. 'Can you see Adz is wrapped in a sheath of light from where the branches have parted overhead?'

Adz grinned as they high-fived to celebrate.

♡♡

As the countdown began to their final post-board days at the boarding school, Adz fled to her 'Baba-zone' often. As often as she touched her jasmine jawline.

She imagined herself as a pogo stick, jumping over reality bites. Or she saw herself assume the form of the mythical Simurg from the Persian fairy tale she read when she was eleven. As if on a trampoline, Adz catapulted into faraway dreams. Like the Amazon River in spate—deep, dark, unstoppable. She and Sanaaya broke into a laugh-fest when her bestie nudged her towards a home truth: her swimming skills were subpar in true time.

Ms Jasmine-bud Face. Ms Warli figure. Ms Cupcakes. Did these names even matter?

On her last day at school, Adz ran past the rose garden. Sadly, emotionally, energetically. Forever memories of wild

Holi celebrations teemed through her mind—feasts of aloo puri and watermelon juice by the jugful. Carnations, phlox, snapdragons and chameli. As she darted past the blooms mindlessly, her big toe snagged on a jagged stone on the unpaved ground.

Adz tumbled. As she struggled to regain her balance, six pairs of hands reached out. Brushing the soil off her bruised right knee, she looked up at a bunch of pre-board faces. One of them wrapped her handkerchief around Adz's knee. Another held her arm and led her to the infirmary. A third picked up Adz's cell phone, dusted off the red soil and handed it back to her.

She looked from face to face, cocooned in a cacophony of warm voices.

'Did you know that we are part of the Adz-Jija fan club?' asked Sumana, one of the pre-boarders.

A strawberry flush washed over Adz's face. Her eyes questioned 'why'.

'Because I heard you speaking up for the handsome gardener Farhan when he was scolded unfairly by grumpy Ms Meenakshi last month. All because he ate cucumbers and radishes off the Marie Curie plot because he had forgotten to pack his rotis and raw onions for lunch on Friday. That took courage, Adz Jija! What if they had expelled you before the boards?' said Bhupinder.

'You may not be the head girl, but you are our heroine,' said Vanitha. 'When I graduate next year, I want to be like you, Adz Jija.'

'Thanks, but find yourselves a better icon soon, will you?' Adz smiled weakly.

Mishi, with her pipsqueak voice, chimed in, 'No way, Adz Jija! I watched you become the sub-junior champ. I want a world like the one you imagined in the debate. I am tiny, like you. You showed me I could be a winner, too.' She paused. 'I watched how you brushed aside those chicken feathers and won for Florence Nightingale house. You won for yourself as well, right?'

'You taught us how to colour outside the lines. And how to be unafraid to own our skins. That's a lot to learn,' Nimisha added with an adoring gaze. 'I wish I had a pretty jasmine bud on my jaw too.'

Mridula butted in, 'Adz Jija, if I have a daughter, I will name her after you . . .'

The juniors gathered around their role model, ready to wrap her in a group hug.

Who could stop Adz? Not even the terrified teenager within her skin. For as Adz befriended herself, her fears fled. She was no longer afraid to lose. For a few seconds every day, she fled her physical frame. She brushed off the chicken feathers, along with a zillion other doubts. Inadvertently, Adz had turned to the light within. And light, she knew, cast no shadows. It flickered forever. From time to time, it even dazzled the world.

HAIR TODAY, GONE TOMORROW

Harshikaa Udasi

'Mario Miranda is super funny. I just saw a cartoon by him about Mumbai monsoons!' said Shanaya.

'Yeah, and he is also so free, like, bold. He shows all the women so curvy!' sniggered Kavya.

The girls burst into giggles. They were poring over a book at Kavya's house. According to some of the parents whose daughters studied at St Pauline Girls' School, Kavya's parents were very broad-minded. They scoffed at helicopter parenting, pooh-poohed when others told them not to let their daughter put on make-up, and were okay with her reading some of their books, which were, as Kavya always said, 'so bold'.

Nandini's eyes fell on a series of cartoons on Bombay. Miss Fonseca *was* curvy, and her boss looked at her in a rather not-nice manner. Yet the things he said made him look silly, in a funny way, and that made Nandini giggle. She quickly turned the page, and that's where she saw it—tucked away in a small section of a cartoon with several stories being told simultaneously. There was a girl with a bright smile, her arms casually thrown behind her head, and a caption that read, 'Hair Today Gone Tomorrow.' Nandini froze. She looked around to see if anyone had seen her look at it. She shut the book and declared, 'Okay, I think I should be off now. It's getting late.'

'Oh, c'mon, Nandini. You live in this very building, just two floors below. You can afford to go a little late. Stay on!' Shanaya yelled.

Nandini shook her head and slipped away. Going down the steps to her house, she wondered if she could ever be that girl in Mario Miranda's comic—smooth hands, smooth legs, smooth underarms, and a smile that didn't curve into hairy ends. Maybe her friends had noticed her knee-jerk reaction. They probably knew the reason for the reaction, too. How could one not notice the black, fuzzy growth that engulfed her whole personality? Snide remarks of 'Hairy Puttar' followed her around at school. *This* hair was a part of her life.

Once home, she retreated to the safe confines of her room. She went up to the mirror and raised her arms. Hidden under the three-quarter sleeves of her salwar kameez, how much of her hands could anyone see? She sighed. Fair skin with dark black hair. How could that ever be concealed? Even the fingers had tiny hairs on them. She could hide her legs all she could by wearing pants and salwars, but what could she do about her hands? If she could thank her stars, it was only for not pasting hair follicles all over her face and neck. Her eyebrows were thick, but not enough to grab attention. Her upper lip, however, had a fair bit of fuzz in the corners. She moved her tongue under her upper lip, pushing up the skin to check if the stubby strands showed. Then she sighed again. The fuzz made her look like her nani, who had chin hair and moustache. *Would she still be this hairy at seventy?* Nandini shuddered at the thought.

'Maybe I will wear only jeans and salwars and track pants my entire life,' she said aloud. But then that terrible thing called a school uniform popped up before her eyes. She loathed the uniform. If there were a competition to rate uniforms, that disgusting navy-blue pinafore with a half-sleeved top would easily rate as the worst-ever uniform design anyone could've imagined. And worse still was that shorter-than-possible white PT skirt that she wore with a mega-sleeved white top on days they had physical training classes.

Her friends saw her every day in her school uniform. Everyone at school saw her. They all saw her legs and hands. Correction. They all saw her hairy legs and hands. Thank god that the nuns were against more skin show and the top wasn't sleeveless. That would have been the ultimate curse.

At assembly every day, Nandini would be aware of girls of the other classes commenting snidely about her legs, because some days her socks would slip down, and the girls were a mean bunch. But Kavya and Shanaya always pulled her out of these messy situations whenever they were around. Oh, how she longed for winter so she could at least put on her cardigan that covered her arms and stylishly flail her cardigan hands. Strangely, the school thought nothing of their shivering legs, so the short skirts and pinafores stayed, and thus did Nandini's woes.

The home wasn't without its set of challenges. And Nandini didn't have Kavya and Shanaya there. Nobody understood how much that stray remark by 'well-meaning' Seema aunty had hurt Nandini. 'Arre *beta*, don't you wipe your body well after a bath? How can young girls have so much hair!' She had said it as though body hair was like grass that grew when watered. Nobody heard Nandini sob into her pillow at night after a family get-together where all the young girls had shown off their trendiest dresses while she sulked in a corner, covered in large, body-hiding clothes.

Her mother would lovingly oil and plait her hair every Sunday morning. 'You know, Nandu, you were born with such a thick, curly mop of hair on your head. In the nursing home, everyone was astonished to see a newborn with such a beautiful head of hair!'

'Maybe they were astonished to see Rapunzel 2.0, with hair all over,' Nandini would mutter. She had seen her baby pictures. She looked like a monkey wearing a wig with blotches of hair on her back and shoulders. The *maalishwaali* aunty had asked her mother to prepare a chana-dal paste in curd with a hint of turmeric daily. It was a story her mom loved to narrate. 'I will remove all this extra hair from your girl's body. When I massage her with this paste, it will all go away,' aunty would say. Her mom had been be infinitely relieved to hear this. Obviously, it hadn't worked.

Her mother, who was normal, as in without much body hair, never seemed to really understand Nandini's terror. 'You don't fret about that. It can be waxed off, sweetie. Just look at your lovely mane. Nobody has such thick hair in the entire colony,' her mother would say encouragingly.

'The last time I tied it up in a ponytail, do you remember those girls called it *ghode ke baal*?' argued Nandini.

Her hair was so thick that when she went for a trim, they would have to tell her stylist to thin it out from the inside. Of course, the hairstylist would 'ooh' and 'aah' over her hair, but they would always have to tip her or him amply for all the extra work.

'Why can't I wax now?' Nandini asked her mother one day. *And thread and bleach*, she thought. She wanted to be normal. Just like other girls. Live life, dress up, be the heart of a party, have Nikhil look at her . . .

'I have said yes. Just wait till your sixteenth birthday. It will coincide with the farewell function at your school. We can't be talking about this all the time, Nandu,' said her mother, tugging her hair. She sounded exasperated. Perspective. That's what it all boils down to. Have you noticed how far off sixteen seems when you're fourteen? And how that proverbial carrot dangled in front of you is also relative.

So, while other girls in her class were being promised make-up kits by Chambor and hair-colouring sessions at Cyril's Salon for the farewell, Nandini was being promised a waxing appointment, along with threading and bleaching at Sujata's Beauty Parlour down the lane. It was going to be a long, long wait. Till then, life did not look smooth. Nandini winced at her choice of words.

A greater ordeal was to begin now, and Nandini dreaded that more than anything else. Post rains, the PT periods shifted from let's-sit-indoors-and-play-chess to sports outdoors. The PT uniforms had to be worn twice a week. For the attractive, smooth-skinned girls of the class—that was 99.99 per cent of the class—PT uniforms meant a chance to show off their toned legs and arms. For the remaining unattractive 0.01 per cent—'that was me,' Nandini woefully remembered—it meant asking mom to open the hem of the skirt so that it extended below her knees. It meant buying the longest socks in the market and pulling them up and holding them with rubber bands so that the leg show was at its minimum.

It was Tuesday, the beginning of a series of dreaded PT periods. How the other girls loved these days! They would roll down their socks or deliberately wear loose ones to show off their never-ending legs. Their skirts looked so smart on them, while Nandini felt like she was lugging a mat around her waist. She walked to her school bus and was soon drawn into the girls' chatter. A new term, a new teacher, a new boy in Reeti's life—there was so much to talk about!

The girls ran up the slope to their classes. None of them heeded Ms Pimenta's warnings of 'girls, in a ladylike manner, please!' Nandini, Shanaya and Kavya took the steps because they needed to go to the staffroom. There, a most unusual sight met Nandini's eyes as Kavya and Shanaya were talking to Ms Khanna. A young girl . . . no . . . a teacher . . . a young teacher was bounding up the steps. Three at a time! Whoa! She could slip. But no, she didn't. She came bounding up, right past Ms Pimenta's disapproving looks. As she caught her breath next to Nandini and noticed that she was being watched, mouth agape and all, she winked at her. Nandini, still stunned, smiled and ran off.

The teacher became the talk of 9C that day, and everyone was curious to know who she was. No teacher of St Pauline's ran up the stairs. Ever. No teacher winked. Ever. They were trained to behave in a ladylike manner. And were expected to train their wards similarly. Nandini thought that besides her own hairy glory, this teacher might be the only other un-ladylike thing to have come within throwing distance of St Pauline.

Shanaya was the first to bring news. 'She's our new Art teacher. Ms Lara left because we were making her crazier than her baby at home. Ta-da, enter Ms Dublina!'

'Hello, girls! Did someone take my name? I am like the devil, you know; think of the devil, and the devil appears!'

a loud voice boomed across the class. It was Ms Runny-Two-Shoes herself. Shanaya scampered to her seat. The rest of them stood rooted in their places.

Finally, someone set alight the class chorus, 'Good morning, Missssss!'

'Yep, good morning and all that. I am your new art teacher because . . .? I have come in during the art class, duh!' she hollered. The only other teacher who hollered was the needlework teacher. Yes, they had one who taught them needlework, and Nandini was awful at it. Hence, Wednesdays equalled hollering. But no one hollered with excitement, and this one seemed to have broken yet another unwritten rule at St Pauline.

The rest of the class was full of general introductions, some terrible arty jokes, an unnecessary speech on art by the hoity-toity Salma, who thought she was next to M.F. Hussain when it came to art, and some pointers on colour mixing. Then, Ms Dublina asked them to draw what they felt like, just about anything. 'But try and be quiet! The quiet part is difficult, but let's try!' she laughed. The girls laughed, Nandini smiled. She liked this one.

Nandini had drawn a beach with unnaturally even waves and a coconut tree leaning too forward into the sea when Ms Dublina appeared next to her.

'Oh dear, I think you might want to straighten up that tree before it crashes into the waves. By the way, they have a lovely rhythm going, your waves. Are they dancing to some music?'

Nandini smiled. Was it her artwork that Ms Dublina was talking about? Ms Dublina held her hand and observed her fingers. 'No wonder. Just look at your lovely fingers! An artist's fingers, these are. Hope you don't go about cracking your knuckles. My granny always said they make your fingers gnarly,' she said, pulling a contorted face.

My fingers? Like an artist's? Did she not see the hair growing out of those very fingers? Nandini glanced at them, wondering if the hair had magically disappeared between the bus ride and now. Zilch luck. Still there, like black grass growing out of parched soil. Yeah, she could even see the tiny holes in her skin from where the hair grew. Follicles, they were called. She learnt that in biology. Ms Dublina had moved ahead to the next girl.

Nandini couldn't concentrate for the rest of the day. When PT period started, she gave her regular stomach-ache excuse and sat under the tree. The coach was picking on girls with inappropriate uniforms. She had picked out about thirteen of them for rolling down their socks and twelve for chalking their shoes to whiten them instead of washing them.

Soon, it was Nandini at the receiving end.

'Others roll down their socks and roll up their skirts. This one wants to open the skirt and make it longer.' The coach pointed at Nandini. 'See how shabby your uniform looks. I want this neatly stitched by the next class. OUT!'

The warning was not half as bad as the danger that lay ahead. Stitch up the skirt? Expose more leg? All those warned were sent off to fetch their almanac for a note to their parents.

'Hey, Nandini. *Ab tu kya karegi?*' It was that annoying Salma again. Had she been a Hindi movie vamp in her previous birth? Salma continued her evil act. 'I mean, short skirt and your hairy legs? You could actually tie plaits on your hands, na? Maybe even on your legs!' She broke into a cackle. Kavya glared at her, ready to explode, and Shanaya let out a laugh . . . Shanaya did WHAT? Nandini looked at Kavya and then at Shanaya. She was nonplussed. Was Shanaya actually laughing? Nandini could not believe it. Kavya glared at Shanaya as Nandini rushed off to the teacher to ask for a washroom break. She could faintly hear Kavya giving Shanaya a dressing down. Tears streaming down her face, she dashed towards the washroom.

'Hello, someone's in a hurry!' It was Ms Dublina. Tears and heartache blurring her vision, Nandini did not see the teacher walk into the washroom that very second.

Nandini was in no mood to see anyone right now—no friend, no Salma, no teacher.

'Hello, young girl! What's the matter? Is all okay in there?' she said, pointing to Nandini's heart.

Nandini burst out crying, and Ms Dublina let her, gently sitting her down on the small chair in the washroom. Once she had stopped sobbing, there was so much Nandini needed to share—so much she had seen, heard and felt. She was okay surviving as a not-beautiful girl, but what she had been handed down was downright ugliness. She sensed the shock every time she met a stranger; the mocking laughter that followed her in the corridors echoed within her.

'Why me, Miss?' Nandini cried, tears welling up once again.

Ms Dublina had only listened so far, without a word, without interrupting. Now, she looked at Nandini earnestly. 'You know, Nandini . . .' she began.

'First, please tell me why you praised my fingers. My fingers are not beautiful. They are hairy, Ms Dublina,' Nandini cut in before her mid-sentence.

'First, sweetheart, tell me what you think of me.'

'You? You are fun, Ms Dublina! You are enthusiastic. You're brave, bold. You . . . you . . . break the rules.'

'Oh, running up the stairs, you mean?' she asked, winking again.

'Yes, and not just that. It is all of you, everything you do. You are also beautiful . . . unlike me.'

'I am beautiful, I know. Thank you. But have you observed me carefully? Look at my hands, Nandini.'

Nandini looked up to see Ms Dublina's hands. Her creamy, white hands, emerging from the sleeveless white dress, were slender and . . . had hair?! But she had never noticed them before! Nandini looked up at Ms Dublina, confusion on her face.

'Do you see the hair? Yes, they have been with me since I was your age, even on my legs. The hair has reduced a little over time, but well, look at them. Ms Dublina swirled around in her pretty white dress. For the first time, Nandini noticed her legs had hair on them. Slightly lighter than hers but in bunches!

'It's not possible at all. You didn't have them earlier.'

'Did I just magically sprout them? No, I always had hair. But you didn't notice because you were too busy noticing that I was—what did you say?—fun, enthusiastic and brave; a rule-breaker and beautiful. Had I not been all of those things, would my hair have been the only thing about me that you would have noticed? Maybe yes, maybe not.'

'When I am your age, will I also have all of these wonderful qualities? Maybe I will. But how does one handle 'now'? Everyone else is Cinderella around here.'

'Well, I had much the same problem. People laughed at me and passed disgusting remarks. I cried, answered back, became a loner, found friends and waxed; well, sometimes I didn't. I learnt to live with my body—hair, pimples and a bunch of whatnots. And look where it's got me? To a lively school with a bunch of lively kids! Life is good. But most of the time I was growing up, I battled it alone, because I didn't have a Ms Dublina. But you, my dear, have me. Importantly, you will be defined by what you do, Nandini. Keep your eyes on that.'

Nandini nodded. She didn't know what to make of all that was said, but she liked the fact that this teacher had her back.

Ms Dublina suddenly looked around, twitching her nose. 'I don't particularly like the smell of this washroom. Do you?'

'No! I don't. I hope you don't plan your next art class here.'

'An arty-farty class, yes!' Ms Dublina gave her a high-five and walked out of the washroom.

Nandini went off to the library. She thought about Ms Dublina. How had she manged to 'live' with her body? Would she too learn? Would Nikhil ever like her with all this hair? Did Nikhil, or for that matter any boy, know that girls also had hair on their bodies? Did Salma also have hair which she got waxed regularly?

She looked at her upper arms, which had comparatively less hair. She wondered if there was a way to graft the skin from there to her forearms and then replicate that all over her body. Copy and replace all. There should be technology to do that. *Maybe I'll invent it*, she thought. *Then I can get on to Shark Tank and get the sharks to invest! Or maybe not . . . who cares? I might as well invent a machine to help people keep their crappy, two-pence-worth opinions to themselves.*

And Nandini laughed.

BEAUTY AND THE BEAST

Vinitha

Once upon a time, a young prince lived in a shining castle. One cold night, an old beggar woman arrived at the castle, offering him a single rose in return for shelter from the cold. Repulsed by her ugliness, the prince turned away from her. Suddenly, she transformed into a beautiful enchantress! To punish the prince for his behaviour, she turned him into an ugly, hideous beast. Then, she gave him a magic mirror and the enchanted rose, telling him it would remain in bloom until his twenty-first year. After that, the rose would wither away, one petal at a time until the last petal. And with that the prince would be gone. To break the spell and reverse his curse, the prince had to love another and earn that person's love before the last petal fell.

Sometimes, when I stand in front of the mirror, I think of the story of *Beauty and the Beast*, and I think of the vain, handsome prince who was turned hideous and had to learn to love himself, thus becoming open to being loved by another. I think of the powerful visual of blood-red rose petals slowly dropping down inside a downturned bell jar, marking the prince's time on earth. He didn't have an eternity, the poor idiot.

I think of all this as I hold a bunch of my hair in my hand and sigh. I'm fifteen, and my hair is falling, much like the rose petals in that bell jar in the fairytale. It is the result of crash diets, I am told. And here I am again, like the prince, evaluating myself in the mirror. Now that I have finally learnt to love myself, pray tell, why are you, my hair, leaving me by the bunch? And how can the thing I now love also be the thing I absolutely hated not too long ago? But I did . . . I did.

All of my middle-school years were spent looking at the mirror and crying about my hair. It was the first—and may I say the only—thing that anyone noticed about me, apparently. My short hair, compressed by a school hairband and school clips, for some reason, invited mirth. I mean, how many times can a person walk into class, stop beside me, point at my hair and say, 'Oh, someone brought Maggi noodles today.' Or look at me and shout out loud, 'Hey, George Bush!' that was followed by the sound of a loud guffaw. Inquisitive minds would walk up to me feigning wide-eyed innocence and ask, 'So Tara, if I put this pencil in your hair, will I ever find it?!' Again, the canned laughter that accompanied these inane sentences was a reminder of how bullies delight in working in groups, and how much time and bandwidth they spend on planned pettiness. When this got boring, they would start inserting pencils, lollipop sticks or pouring tinsel and thermocol balls on my hair. I imagine I made school quite the learning experience for a lot of my classmates.

So, needless to explain more, I hated my short hair. I let it grow out, thinking that would do the trick. Nothing changed. Things actually got worse. Every morning began with my daily torture session that I called 'Taming-of-the-Hair'. My super curly hair would be combed, untangled, divided and straitjacketed into two tight plaits, which most ICSE schools demanded (perhaps still do) of girls. What can I say?

Even if there was a whole hour to do this—and my mom never had more than two minutes—untangling curly hair required expertise, gentleness and NOT CURLING-NESS! So, my hair would be stretched, torn, fought and conquered. Mom chanting 'Sorry! Sorry! Sorry!' at regular intervals as she conducted this unintended torture, didn't help. I cried my way through the ordeal, only to go to school and wade my way through unending jeering remarks as I held back bitter tears.

What do you do when you are constantly the butt of bushy jokes—every hour, every day, every week, every month, month after month? You learn to join in. I wasn't doing myself any favours by being the 'sensitive girl', so I thought I'd be the 'class-clown girl'. It worked. I laughed, everyone laughed. Did the internal wincing stop? Did the internal wincing reduce? What do you think?

The most popular question asked of me was, 'Have you ever tried straightening it?' I probably would have in a heartbeat. In fact, the one time—I was twelve—when my aunt ironed my hair with a pair of tongs for a cousin's wedding was the happiest day of my pre-teen life. Even after the function was over, I didn't want to wash my hair, and I would have stayed like that forever if the wonderful Mumbai moisture hadn't done its evil thing. By the end of the day, thanks to the *shaadi-wala* crowd and profuse sweating, my straightened hair had morphed into limp curls and then swiftly snapped back into a wiry mop. Ugh!

So, when my mom gave in to my pitiful crying and took me to a parlour to get my hair straightened for my thirteenth birthday, it was pure, undiluted happiness.

From floating in imagined happiness about slow-motion walking into school with straight, shiny-as-polished-glass hair and everyone gasping at how awesome I looked, I came crashing down to the wretched reality—the salon women refused. I was underage, apparently. I wasn't eligible for chemicalized, permanent hair straightening. What they could do was cut and blow-dry my hair. Bah! I know how the zapped, horrified prince must have felt. I knew his despair then.

I turned fourteen. Curly haired, bespectacled. Did I tell you I was considered stout? Braces were added to the beast, and with a loud clang, the life sentence was sounded. Who would ever love this beast? Even when I became resigned to having curly hair, I still felt like and was an awkward teenager. This story had no background music, and the girl did not get the guy or a cool new friend group. I don't know how the curly-haired goddesses on the Internet do it. How do they always look so amazing and ethereal? I still very much felt like a girl with frizzy hair.

Then, the COVID-19 pandemic happened. The peace of being at home and less bullied allowed me to diet and lose weight. Did distance do the trick? I'll never know. But, two years later, when the doors were cautiously opened and people started meeting in real-time, I found that my hair was once again the only thing people noticed. Only this time, it was to say absurdly nice things about it. I still don't understand it. It was like Sleeping Beauty went to sleep, and when she woke up, she found that a hundred years had passed and the only thing that had been mocked about her was suddenly uber cool. In any case, my hair became the thing people noticed about me. *Hey, I'm Tara. I have lovely nails, I make amazing art, my dry humour is something you'll always notice in my writing* . . . but no, it was only my hair.

So, did the beast finally learn to love herself? After all, that is her ticket to the 'Happy Ending', right? But no. The road to self-love is not a straight one. It comes with its twists.

Everyone loves my hair now, and it is the same hair they all had made fun of not so long ago. And no, I still feel like an awkward and gawky teenager (just a year older) and nowhere close to the dazzling, shiny curly-haired goddesses of the Internet. But now, because my hair is the one thing people compliment me on, it has become my new insecurity. So, whenever I have to step out of the house now, I make sure to start prepping my hair three hours in advance. Washing alone takes at least an hour. Drying and scrunching it with leave-on conditioners take the other two hours. Which means I can now never leave the house to go anywhere without making sure my hair looks absolutely perfect.

I'm invited to events, but my going there is not dependent on my social calendar. Rather, it depends on whether I am too tired to wash my hair then. No wash equals cancelled plans.

Is my hair the only beautiful thing about me now? If I lost that would I no longer be attractive? I wonder as I stand in front of the mirror, looking at myself, looking at my hair. I've lost weight, thanks to eating frugally, swimming for an hour and running for tuition. But I'm losing my hair as well. The bathroom drain bears witness, and there is evidence stuck in the bristles of my hairbrush. Worry tightens my chest.

Mom is exasperated when she oils my hair. 'You better eat properly,' she says. 'You are losing hair.'

In the mirror in front of me, I see someone in a fitted top and pants. My clip-on nose ring glints as I shift my weight on my feet. The high heels accentuate my curves and my height. I straighten myself and walk closer to the mirror. My eyes meet my eyes in the reflection and soften their gaze.

I'm learning slowly to make peace with everything about myself. I can't say I feel a sense of contentment, yet with that knowledge comes the acceptance that I suppose I never will. But on my good days—they rarely come by—I can hear both the good and the mean things people say about my hair. I sit with it and feel what I feel.

The fairy tale was quite right. I think of the prince trapped inside the body of a beast, with his self-loathing, and how nothing changed for him. And I think of how he learnt to love—first himself and then her—and how it changed everything.

As long as people have the ability to voice their opinions, they will continue to do so. But on the good days, these comments don't touch me. I am so grateful for my good days. On these days, I tell myself that it's time to love ourselves as we are. Because when we do, everything—all the mean comments, all the bullying and the adulation—falls by. No one will need rescuing then, beast or no beast. And I remind myself: Who knows what Beauty's story was? Who knows which part of her she felt anxious about?

THE SMELL OF EARTH

Shals Mahajan

The paint flakes
      under my fingers
to reveal the soft layer
      of plaster of Paris
      on top of the cemented
           hardness

I dig at it
scooping bit by tiny bit
in little half-moons inside
my nail

To empty it in
      swift unhurried
      almost absent-minded
motions

       to my waiting mouth
       my aching teeth

These walls are marked by me
       in my own special way
Do not think anyone even notices
       this writing on the walls

This writing of my nails
This writing of my want
Of my ache and my clenching
Writing so hard
       so often
             that my nails are torn . . .

On days that I am alone
       I dig with my compass
I make little packets of pieces
wrapped in newspaper bits
       for later

I know construction well
I know where to dig
       to lay open the vein of riches

THE SMELL OF EARTH

The joints that are softer
The edges that are harder

Masons who built these walls
And I
Have much in common

I see walls and I know which ones
are cemented and which
are layered over with
plaster of Paris

And the best of them
those that are plastered
with choona (lime) and sand

They crumble in chunks
into my waiting hands
and taste what earth tastes like

Earth is not food
It is a necessity

I eat it through the walls
through pieces of chalk

till my mouth is filled
with slowly dissolving grit

I eat till I feel coated by clay
And then I am done

A layer of peace descends over me
A layer of need satisfied

Something fulfilled
Something found

Taste texture smell
all satiated

Craving is that which is
engraved on the walls
that which is spit
through a mouthful
of remaining sand

Craving is the smell of earth
when the first rain falls

And if I can't eat that smell
I will not live.

DARKEN MY KAJAL

Suha Riyaz Khopatkar

Her timer was set.

Eight minutes is all she takes to shower every day.

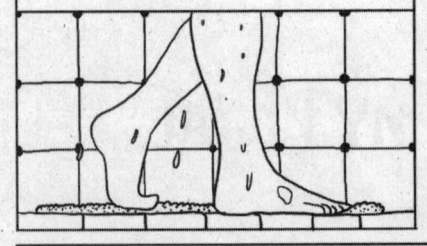

With her hair wrapped in a towel, she wraps another around herself and goes to the mirror.

She has a strict skincare routine to follow.

As always, the mirror is foggy. It needs a good wipe.

But the steam from the shower is crucial for three out of her **Fifteen-Step Beauty Regimen.**

The key is to apply all products in upward strokes. It lifts your skin and avoids early sagging, so she'd heard in several skincare tutorials.
At fifteen, she holds the record amongst her classmates for not getting even a single pimple since fifth grade.
She has to leave the house soon if she is to get to school before the creepy watchman closes the gates. He lets her sneak in even after the bell rings . . .
. . . whenever she asks nicely.

> The school uniform left a few windows to personalize one's look. With or without a note from the class monitor, she kept experimenting.

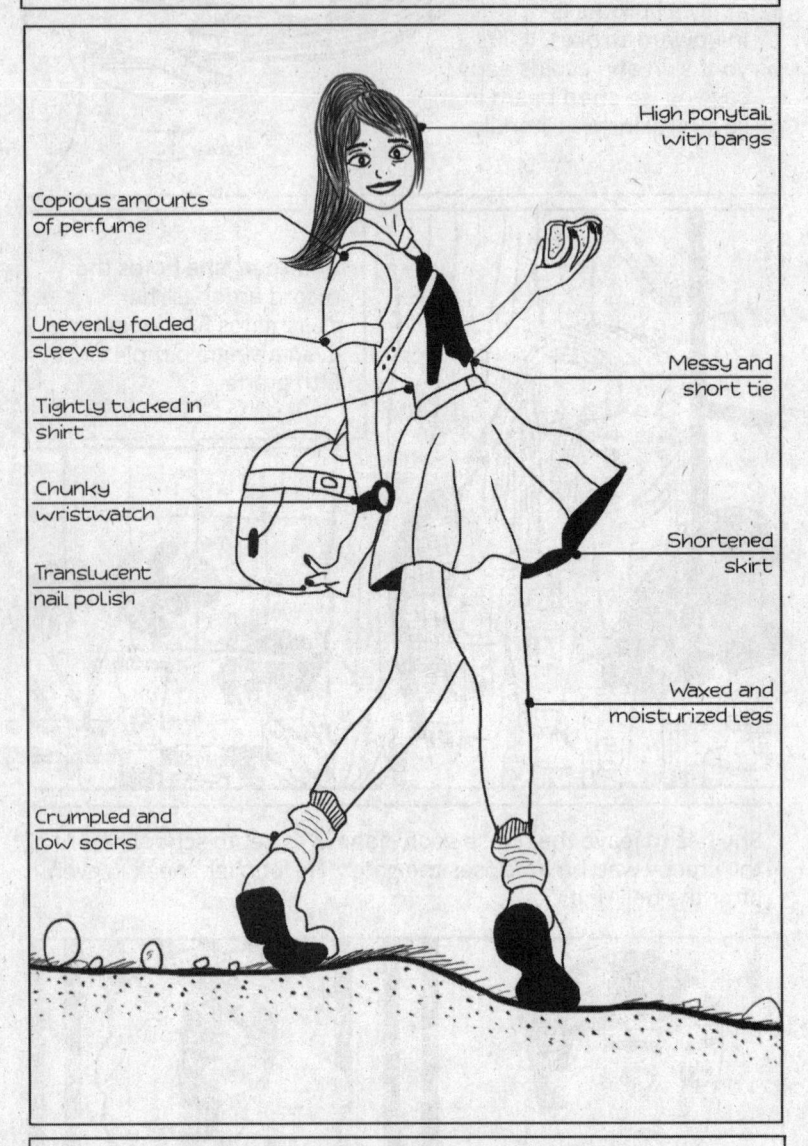

- High ponytail with bangs
- Copious amounts of perfume
- Unevenly folded sleeves
- Tightly tucked in shirt
- Chunky wristwatch
- Translucent nail polish
- Messy and short tie
- Shortened skirt
- Waxed and moisturized legs
- Crumpled and low socks

> She slings her bag across her body, grabs a slice of bread with Nutella and is off to school.

DARKEN MY KAJAL

The route is set. It's a seventeen-minute walk to her school. Twenty-five, if she finds herself a worthy adventure.

... entangled electrical wires and

She looks up when she walks, to notice bizarre things...

cats stuck on tree branches.

Once, she saw a pigeon flying with kite string entangled around its foot.

She had chased the bird for ten minutes, trying to spare it from its misery, but somehow, it flew across buildings and out of her sight. She carried the bird's pain with her all day. But she never let it show on her face. To others, she was her usual, perky self.

93

Everyone sees her the same way. Beauty. Oh, and what a beauty she is! More than her flawless skin and symmetrically aesthetic face, it is her eyes that glow. And they all see it.

They notice her as soon as she enters their field of vision. She loves it too—the attention.

In fact, she prefers meeting new people more than hanging out with the same old friends in their same old hangouts.

← Pappu Can't Dance Saala

Yo!! Let's go outttt ✦

I wana go for pikuzz today. In?? Pls don't do drama today Shail... 😊

We gotta do shakes after as well I told Suzi that I'd show her our OG Shake Shack... 💯 ⚡

yep! 🎉 💯 🔥 ❄️ 🖤🖤

Gr8 m cmng frm classes dnt w8 4 me ill b dr asap 💨

not tonigh|

← We Gon EEEAAATT!!

hi all! We meeting 2day?

sureeee sureee anyone wanna suggest a place?

can I get a couple of friends frm Colony to hang? Cool wid all? Lmk

Ya man! N I dnt knw any places here... ✖

all I wanna do is sit and eat smthng super duper cheeeeessyyyyyyyy. Dazz all. 🎭

Pizza! Pizza! Pizz|

She loves to enter new rooms. Meet new people. She looks forward to it. They love her energy and charm. She lets them.

We should go dancing together!

GoGo Go

That's the best new ay to keep fit

DANCE to

What do you even eat?!

WOOHOO !!

LOOK at HER

Where does she get her energy from?

WoW

I wanna learn to dance like that!

OooO LALA

you can take classes for sure!

He was her maths teacher.

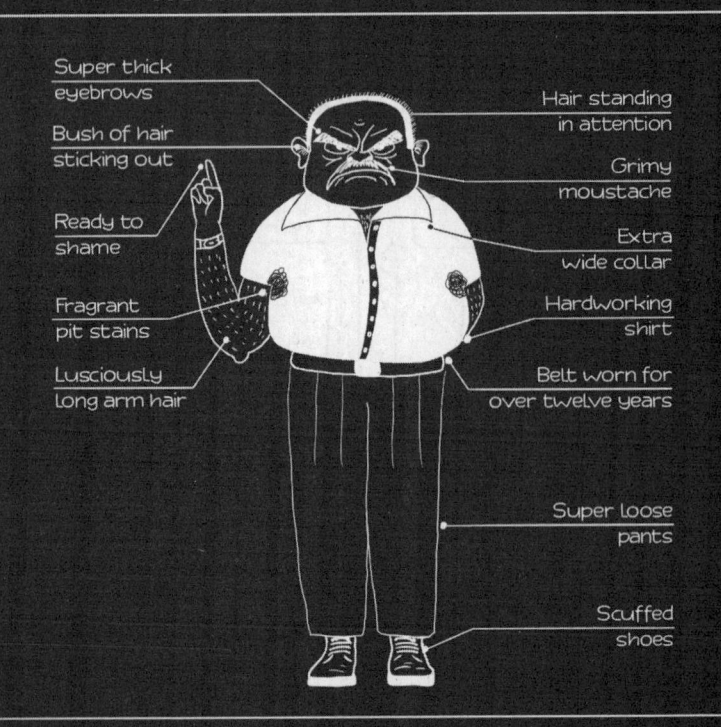

- Super thick eyebrows
- Bush of hair sticking out
- Ready to shame
- Fragrant pit stains
- Lusciously long arm hair
- Hair standing in attention
- Grimy moustache
- Extra wide collar
- Hardworking shirt
- Belt worn for over twelve years
- Super loose pants
- Scuffed shoes

Well-reputed and stern. Everyone feared him. But he had a soft side that rarely anyone got to see.

"listen to me..."

"you call this a tie?!"

"see you in class."

He treated her different. Nice at times, encouraging her acumen.

And mean at times, commenting on her uniform improvisations.

But always too close for comfort... she had learned to steer clear of him.

She tried to keep her head down and not talk much during his class, just to avoid his gaze. He often pointed out that she required extra tutoring and she should join his after-school tuitions, but she never did.

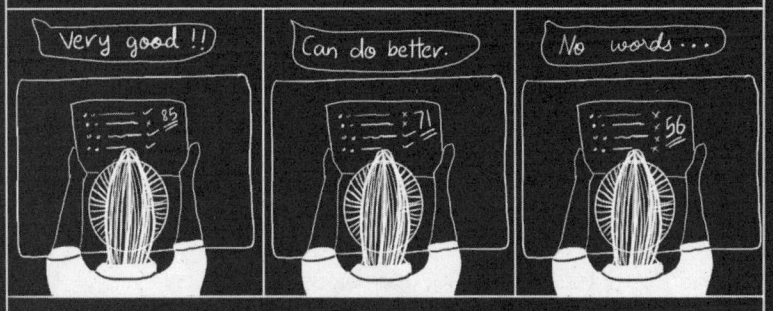

Very good !!	Can do better.	No words...
85	71	56

Her scores were suffering, but she would just . . .

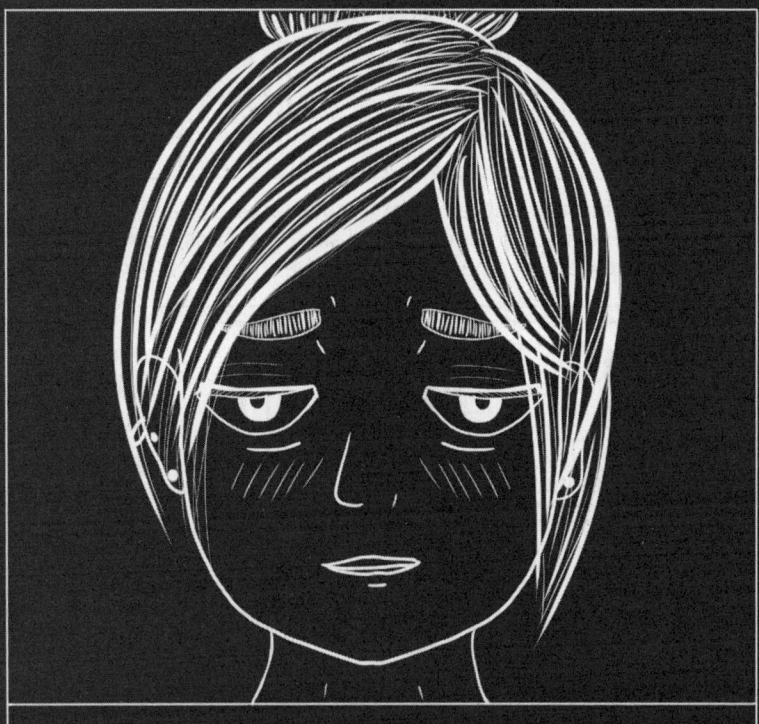

. . . look up at a random detail, and it would drift her away from the events on ground.

There is an ant circling in her shower. It is standing its ground, even with the hot water streaming so close to it.

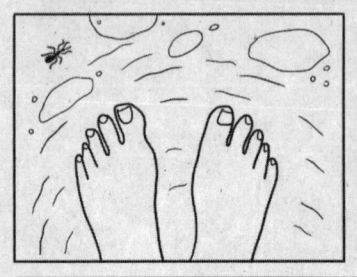

She pauses in front of the mirror for a moment. She wipes off the steam and skips a couple of her skincare steps today. Nothing changed. It's fine. She needn't be this excessive anyway.

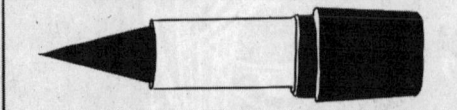

She tried a new kajal. It looks good; she could get into trouble at school . . .

. . . but she can always wash it off, so she keeps it on and slips into her football jersey.

She does a couple of turns in front of the mirror. It's okay, not too tight; should work for practice.

Sports practice is in the evenings. She never misses a single day. She is always equipped with her sports kit at school.

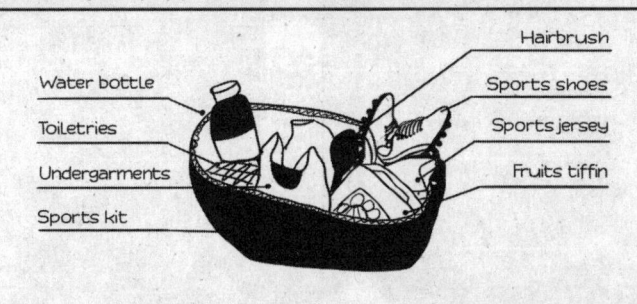

- Water bottle
- Toiletries
- Undergarments
- Sports kit
- Hairbrush
- Sports shoes
- Sports jersey
- Fruits tiffin

Her mind likes to move, and so does she.

woohoo!

The ground feels like home. She likes to dissolve into the ground along with her sweat.

He appears out of nowhere.

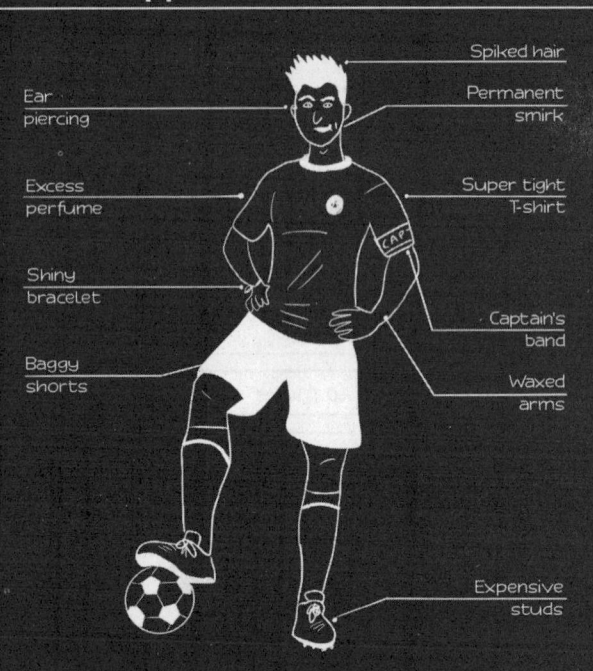

- Spiked hair
- Ear piercing
- Permanent smirk
- Excess perfume
- Super tight T-shirt
- Shiny bracelet
- Captain's band
- Baggy shorts
- Waxed arms
- Expensive studs

As if he's been waiting for her to show up. He has been playing for the boys' football team for four years now. Most of the girls in the class have a crush on him. He is obnoxiously loud.

> Somebody's brought their A-game!

He is complimenting her plays. She ignores him.

> You got This!

He keeps following her around the ground.

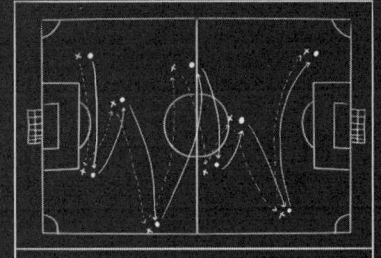

He pops up again with unwanted tips. Sometimes it's easier to pretend that she can't hear him.

She can feel him running behind her, coming closer. She turns around to look when . . .

SNAP!

. . . her knee jerks forward and she twists her ankle badly!

Now on bed rest, she is left to observe her bedroom's ceiling for a week. She should redo the mural on her ceiling that she'd painted. It has stopped surprising her.

Now fully recovered and done with exams, it is time to relax. She bounces off her bed and starts working out. The hot shower post workout feels great on her sore muscles.

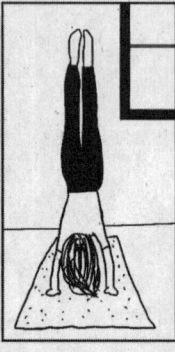

With the board exam results still a month away, her mornings are lazy. She slashes a few more steps from her morning skincare routine.

She notices dark circles under her eyes, but it could also be the unwashed kajal from a few days back. Instead of wiping it off, she applies a fresh coat. The smoky-eye look should work for tonight. It was the party of the year—**Post Exams Bash!**

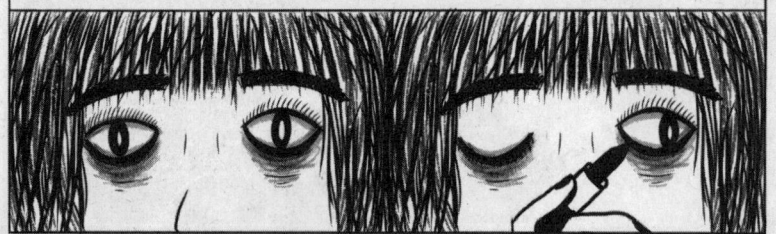

She usually hates parties. They are always at a loud, dark club where the seniors from school help her friends with the entry.

SPEAK UP!

Say that again!

Is Jinal here yet?

What are you saying?

HAVE YOU SEEN SHUBHAM?

HUH?!

Dressed as a twenty-something-year-old at fifteen, she looks older than her age. One can tell by the way she wears her kajal.

She loves to dance. She can get lost in the rhythm and not care about her surroundings. She dissolves away, especially when she's surrounded by her girlfriends.

She rarely touches a drink but gets mistaken for a girl-who-knows-her-alcohol quite often. She wonders why.

He asked her for a recommendation.

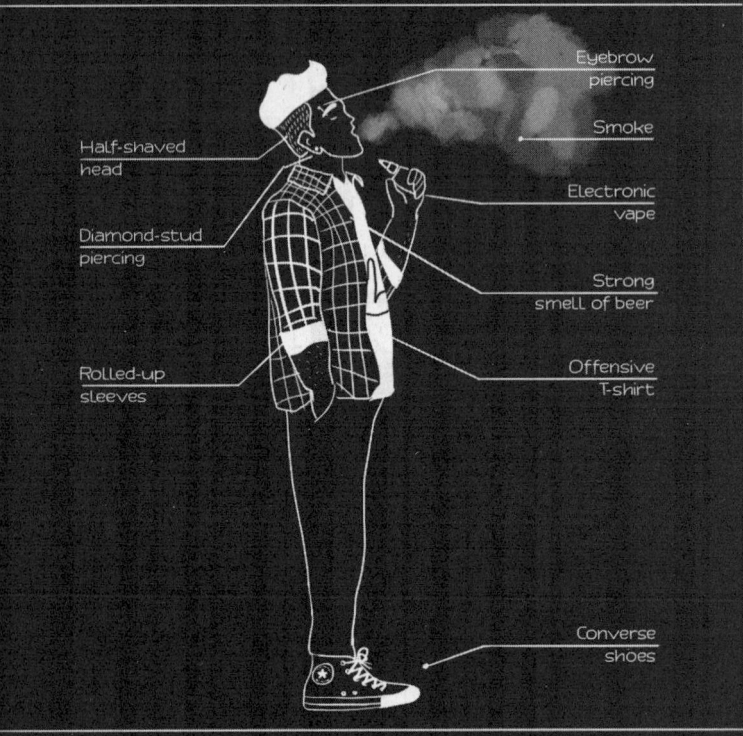

- Eyebrow piercing
- Smoke
- Half-shaved head
- Electronic vape
- Diamond-stud piercing
- Strong smell of beer
- Rolled-up sleeves
- Offensive T-shirt
- Converse shoes

"I need something stronger..."

She looked at him puzzled. Who was he? Oh, a friend of a friend of a friend, he explained. She was polite, not revealing how clueless she was.

He clearly had no problem consuming considerable amounts of alcohol without anyone's suggestion as he could barely stop grinning. So why was he asking?

DARKEN MY KAJAL

He kept smiling and telling her that she looked good while dancing, and then suddenly grabbed her from behind.

She kept looking for the unusual on the ceiling, but it was dark and all she could see were spinning lights from the rotating disco ball. The lights were dancing freely. Unlike her.

That did it, she couldn't dissolve anymore.

People exhaust her.

She's taking a day off from them and redoing her room. Stroke by stroke, her ceiling mural is turning out quite well. The sketch was cluttered with a lot of women, not a single man in sight. Her mind was drifting away. Wandering.

She could never be friends with a boy. He would want something more.

A light touch, a wrong glance, a well-timed smirk or a cheeky line.

Like she owed him something. Like she asked him to come closer to her. Make a move . . .

3:45
Alarm- Crochet-ting

OMG! I have class TODAY!

DARKEN MY KAJAL

She has to get ready for her crochet classes! She's late already. Her room is a mess. She hasn't cleaned or used any of her skincare products lately. Her skin would just have to cope, like her.

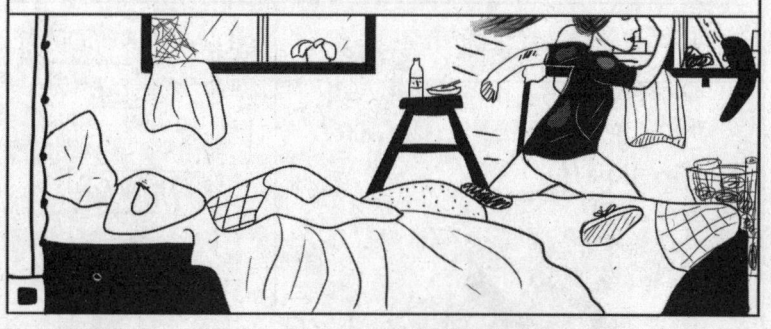

Her kajal is refusing to budge even after multiple wipes. She can't tell where her kajal ends and where her eyes begin.
It angers her.
She is furious.
Can she not see her own eyes?
Is that even possible?!

uhhh!!

Did you shrink? AAA!!

UGHH!

Nothing is fitting right. Everything clings to her body. The mirror is highlighting her curves. This is what others see.

She runs to her closet and starts rummaging through her clothes. There's a pile on the floor, but the hunt is on.

Her parents call out to her, asking her about all the ruckus. They are completely clueless of the storm that lives within her.	She doesn't bother to respond as she has found **THE ONE!**

"BETA! What's going on in there?! You okay?"

"STOP with all that noise!"

"IT'S PERFECT!"

FUNNY GIRL

She slips it on. It doesn't cling to her and hangs loosely five inches below her butt. She immediately feels at ease.

FUNNY GIRL

She sees what they'd see. The eyes wouldn't penetrate through this. She feels protected. She didn't feel like herself though . . . She grabs her bag and rushes out.

DARKEN MY KAJAL

She stands on the street with her arm out, impatiently waiting for an autorickshaw. Luckily, one comes to a screeching halt.

RICKSHAA!

STOP

Just as she is stepping into the autorickshaw, within a fraction of a second, she feels an arm graze along her back. She freezes.

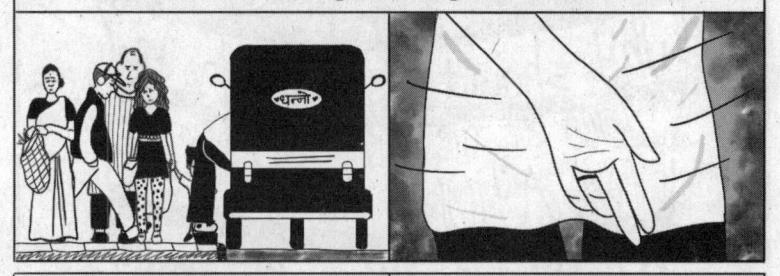

Goosebumps
raise the hair on her body!

Sirens
blare in her head!

She springs back to spot the pervert . . .

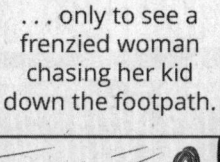

. . . only to see a frenzied woman chasing her kid down the footpath.

Her body eases up . . .

. . . only to wonder . . .

109

Why should I change who I am?
HOW COME NOT-SO-NICE MEN HAVE A HOLD ON MY MIND?
Why am i filled with Shame?
HOW IS THIS MY FAULT?
Why am I so scared?
NO MORE LIVING IN FEAR!

She hops into the autorickshaw.

Takes a deep breath and relaxes her shoulders.

Opens her hair as the autorickshaw rattles on.

Knots her T-shirt. Smiles.

And she rides off looking up at the bright sky.

COLOUR BAR

Smita Vyas Kumar

Shweta and Vikram had just finished dinner when Malini called.

'Hey, Princess! How's it going?'

'Totally crazy, Mals. This new division launch is leaving me breathless. Today was the first time in ten days that I could have dinner with Vikram.'

'Aww, you poor overworked, overpaid thing. Good ol' Manisha holding fort at home?'

'Yes, she is in charge. But Vikram is the true rockstar here. He's not only looking after Taru but also doing son-in-law duty.'

'Oh, your parents are visiting.'

'They came last week. It's too cold in Delhi.'

'So, Princess is getting her face packs?'

'One every other night.' Shweta rolled her eyes and smiled.

'I'll come to meet them soon. *Achha*, guess who called me today?'

'George Clooney.'

'I wish. No, Madhavi Rana.'

'What? That horrid girl. Why? I hope you hung up on her.'

'Shwets, it's been twenty-five years since we left school. About time you got over the whole thing. Please listen to your wisest and oldest friend.'

'Go on, tell me.'

'This is our school's fiftieth year, and a big celebration has been planned for Founder's Day. The Alumni Association is felicitating ten outstanding students at a gala dinner, and you, my dear, are one of the ten.'

'Oh really? That's nice.'

Malini continued. 'You have become famous since you won the Business Times Marketing Whiz Award as the youngest marketing head at an MNC worldwide. Madhavi is the Secretary this year. She asked me to ask you if you would go to the event.'

Madhavi's face flashed in Shweta's head, and her expression darkened. 'Why couldn't she ask me herself?'

'I guess she knew you wouldn't take her call. Shweta, you are a grown-up woman who is talking like a teenager. Let it go. It will be a fun evening! Most of our class will be there.'

'Including the "gang of four"?'

'Yes.'

'I'm not going then.'

'Just sleep over it. That's all I'm saying. *Chalo*, good night, Princess.'

Shweta peeped into Tara's bedroom. Her seven-year-old was fast asleep. Later, as she lay in bed, trying to wind down, she felt restless, a growing unease. The thought of seeing the gang of four had dropped a heavy stone in her heart.

Vikram walked in a little later.

'Is Taru okay?' She asked him.

'She is fine. She knows you are busy with "very impotent work", as she calls it.' Then he looked at her and paused. 'You look upset,' he said. 'What happened?'

She told him about the dinner-and-award event. 'I feel stupid. I know it is silly, yet I can't help it. How can a bunch of schoolmates still have such a hold over me?' she asked herself, even as she asked him. She examined herself in the mirror and smiled. The years had been generous to her. Her health gleamed through her flawless, fair complexion.

'You look great, Shwets,' Vikram said and smiled reassuringly.

I know I do, she thought, allowing herself a self-congratulatory moment. *I wish I felt the same way, too.*

'Want to tell me about this gang of four?' Vikram asked, sitting down next to her on the bed. As she sank into the cool pillow covers, Shweta's mind travelled back in time.

'It all started around the time I was in the ninth grade, I remember. Until then, life was pretty good. I was Li'l Miss Popular back in primary school. Girls would fight each other just to carry my schoolbag from the bus to the classroom. There would be someone carrying my water bottle during recess, and someone else would fetch me snacks from the canteen.'

'Woah! Who does such stuff? You must have been quite a bully.'

'Not at all. If anything, I was quite mild-mannered. The teachers loved me because I was obedient and did my homework. Maybe that rubbed off on the girls.'

'Still, I think there must have been something more to it,' Vikram said.

'Well, I was a cute-looking kid as well.' Shweta smiled. 'You have seen my childhood photos, right?'

'Yes. A fair, round face, cute button eyes and brown hair in two long braids. And you still have that same enchanting smile,' Vikram said with a smile.

'Ha, ha, ha! Thanks!' Shweta felt a bit better. 'The teachers loved me and chose me for every extra-curricular activity: singing, dancing, elocution, you name it. I went to all the inter-school competitions. I always got to perform the solo number in singing competitions, and I was always the princess in the school plays. That's how I got the nickname, Princess.'

'Then what happened to all the adulation?'

'I don't know, Vikram. The whispers started when I was in senior school. There was gossip about how the teachers loved me only for my fair complexion; they singled me out even though I was not a talented or intelligent student. Some of the girls made fun of the way I walked, the way I tied my hair . . . everything about me was wrong.'

Shweta paused to take a breath. It had been ages, but the faces came back to her like it had all happened yesterday. The hateful gang of four, as she had named them: Swati, Leena, Madhavi and Anju. How they would look through her even when she tried talking to them. How they would mimic her voice every time they passed her in the corridors.

'The gang started a hate campaign against me. They spread a rumour that the teachers gave me high marks because they were besotted with me. According to them, I didn't deserve to stand first in class, Madhavi did because she was the truly intelligent one. But because of me, she was always passed over by the teachers.'

Vikram was aghast. 'That's a pathetic excuse. You are an all-India board ranker!'

'Yes, but that was later. In ninth grade, I was so miserable that I did badly in all the exams and wasn't even among the top three in class. They were so thrilled they threw a party for Madhavi in recess for defeating the princess.'

'My poor Shwets! How much you have suffered.'

'It just kept getting worse. During the head-girl elections, they made sure no one campaigned for me. I just had Malini and two other friends, who were the quiet types, supporting me. Ma stayed up all night and made 'Vote for Shweta' placards, but there was no one to carry those placards, except for me and my three friends. It was so embarrassing, sitting in class with the pile of placards. Of course, I lost. They took out a victory march for Madhavi and openly laughed at my face when they passed me. I can't bear to think of it, Vikram.'

He gave her some water to drink. She gulped it down.

'On our annual day, I won the Ms Vidya Niketan Contest. I was so happy! Malini and I were just about to walk into our classroom when we overheard the gang discussing the contest. I still remember the conversation . . .' Her voice wobbled a bit.

'As expected, the princess became the queen. What a damp squib!' Swati said, shaking her head.

Leena said, 'Teacher's darling after all. I don't know why I even bothered to get a new outfit and call a makeup person. I was sure I had a chance.'

'I honestly don't know what they see in her. It's not like she is pretty. She is just fair. Her eyes are so close, she looks squinty. And that long, lank hair. Ughh! And her fingers are short. Not artistic at all.' Madhavi grotesquely folded her fingers.

'Even her nose is flat like a pig's. Hey, we should call her Princess Piggy,' said Swati, and the group burst into laughter.

Shweta felt her tears welling up again, just as they had that day.

'They called me a pig, Vikram. A pig. I cried alone in my room every day after school that last year.'

'Why didn't you tell Ma and Papa? They could have helped you.'

'NO! Ma would have complained to the school authorities. The teachers would have come down heavily on these girls, and then what would happen to me? Malini was my island of sanity. I can never thank her enough. I still don't know what I did to these girls to deserve this treatment.'

Vikram held her hand and pressed it gently. 'You all became adolescents with raging hormones, Shwets. It happens. You have to get over it. Think of this instead. You topped your school in the board exams. You went to an IIM and got a gold medal!' He grinned as he hugged her and said, 'And you married a wonderful man. Forget these girls.'

'I had stashed all this away, somewhere deep in my mind. This call today brought it all back. Don't think I can go back to school and see them again.'

'I think you should go. I would love to see their faces when you go up on stage to get your award. But it's really up to you. Now, in other news, Taru's annual day is coming up. She is all excited.'

'Of course, she will be. After all, she has my genes.' Shweta smiled. Discussing Tara always relaxed her.

The next day was a whirlwind of meetings. Shweta saw two missed calls from her mom and called back.

'All okay, Ma?'

'Yes, all fine. Just wanted to know what time you will be home. Don't work too late. You will get dark circles. How will you look on stage when you receive your award?'

'Ma, please. Stop it. First of all, I haven't decided if I am going. Second, they are not rewarding my looks, but my achievements. I'll talk to you later.' She knew she was being brusque, but the last thing she needed was an argument with her mother about dark circles and fair complexion.

Shweta's fair complexion had become a point of conflict with her parents. As a child, she loved the attention and the compliments: 'such an angel', 'all colours suit you', 'skin like marble'. But as an adult, her complexion became an obstacle in her path to achieving her dreams. Her parents wanted her to get married right after graduation. 'While your beauty is in full bloom,' her mother had said.

But Shweta wanted to study, and work. She took the IIM entrance exam secretly, and when she got through to IIM, Lucknow, she presented her parents with her acceptance letter. All hell had broken loose.

'So far away! And two years all alone in a new city?' Her dad argued.

'But Papa, it's IIM! And I'll be living in a hostel with others. Besides, Lucknow is a big city.'

Her mother countered with a new argument. 'Big or small, fair women are targets everywhere.'

'Ma, I can take care of myself. Also, any woman, whatever her colour, can be a target. I am not unique in that.'

'What do you know? Fair girls attract more attention. I know how the boys at the corner tease you. They call you 'milk bottle', right?'

Shweta was aghast. 'Ma, you knew, and you didn't say a word to their parents?' She had been too afraid to tell Ma and Papa about this teasing, lest they stop her from going to college, but her mother had known about it . . . and done nothing!

'I didn't want to create a ruckus. People would have spoken ill of you. We can't risk your reputation.'

'This is so unfair. I have to suffer when it's not my fault. You want me to sit in a dark room to keep my white skin unblemished and your reputation safe? I may as well drop out of life.' Shweta had cried all night in self-pity. Her fair skin was a curse. That day, she decided she would choose her path and be in control of her own life.

Her parents' euphoria when Shweta was awarded the gold medal as the batch all-rounder at IIM Lucknow was short-lived. Her mother was livid when she got a sales job at a multinational.

'Walking about in the sun from one *kirana* store to another, what kind of job is this? You'll get tanned horribly! How will you find a good match?'

But Shweta had stuck to her guns and gone off on long tours, her bag full of her mother's anti-tan face packs, a peace settlement.

The phone rang, and Shweta sighed. Before her meeting began, she sent off a quick message to Malini: 'I don't think I'll attend the bash, Malini. Not up to it.'

The next day was Friday. Shweta decided to wrap up early and get some 'Mamma-Tara time'.

She entered her home and yelled, 'Surprise!'

Her mom said, 'Thank god you are home. I was about to call you. Taru is refusing to come out of her room. She has been there ever since she came back from school. She didn't want her favourite nachos or to go down and play. I don't know what's wrong.'

Worried, Shweta entered Tara's room and switched on the light. Tara was sleeping curled up, the prickly-heat powder box next to her. She had dabbed it on her arms and legs. Was she ill?

'Taru baby, are you okay?' Shweta stroked her head gently.

Tara turned around. Two dark eyes looked out of a face caked with powder as well.

'Why so much powder, Taru? Is your skin itching? Shall I call Doctor Uncle?'

'I'm fine, Mamma. I'm trying to become fair like you.'

'Why darling?' asked Shweta, shocked by Tara's revelation.

'Sangeeta Miss didn't make me the princess in the annual-day play. She said I didn't look the part.'

'That's okay, darling. Whom did she choose?'

'Who else, Mamma? That same stupid Sia Kumar. They take her for everything just because she is fair. She didn't even remember the dialogues. I knew them by heart, and still she chose Sia.'

'Maybe Sia had better expressions?' Shweta ventured, trying to validate the teacher's decision.

'Mamma, why are you taking her side? Do you also hate me because I'm not fair like you? Do you also think Sia should get all the chances in everything, just because she is all pink? Sangeeta Miss never looks at me. It is always Sia this and Sia that.'

Tara started crying, her tears making little rivulets in the powder. Shweta's heart sank as she pulled Taru into her arms and hugged her tight. 'No, no darling, never. You are the most important person in my life. I am always on your side, I promise. Tell me, did you get a role in the play?'

'Yes. Miss made me the Magic Talking Tree.'

'That sounds like a fun thing to be. A Magic Talking Tree!'

'I don't want to be a tree, Mamma,' Tara wailed. 'I want to wear the princess gown and crown and sit on the throne.'

Shweta took Tara on her lap and rocked her till she stopped crying. She stroked Tara's head to soothe her.

Tara asked very softly, 'Are you my stepmother, Mamma? The girls in the class said my real mother died and then Papa married you. My real mamma was my colour. Is that true?'

Shweta sat up with a start. She gathered her wits about her quickly. 'Of course not! Don't you remember seeing photos of me with my big tummy when you were inside it? I'll show you again, look.' She fished out the pregnancy photos on her phone. 'Guess who is in my tummy, kicking me?' she said and smiled.

'Mamma, did you drink coffee when I was in your tummy? Granoo said drinking coffee makes you dark. Maybe . . . that's why I am not like you.' Tara's eyes were questioning.

'Not at all!' Shweta blurted out, startling Tara. Then she quickly softened her tone. 'You see, Granoo doesn't always know everything. Maybe she was told the wrong things when she was in school, no? I will explain everything to her. Children can look like their mamma or daddy. You came out looking like daddy because you are his favourite. You know that, right?'

Tara nodded vigorously. 'Yes. I am daddy's doughnut.'

'And see what a lovely chocolate doughnut you are! I am so hungry; I want to eat my chocolate doughnut,' Shweta said as she made pretend-biting faces.

Tara giggled.

'Okay, now tell me about the Magic Talking Tree. What do you have to say?'

'I have to say, "abracadabra!" and wave my arms,' said Tara excitedly. But then her eyes grew sad again. 'The princess has lots of dialogue.'

'Don't worry about the princess. Let's make you the *bestest* Magical Talking Tree they have ever seen. Everyone will notice how fantastic you are and remember your role for days. How should we make the costume?'

'Let's have blue leaves!' Tara's imagination took over.

'We can get Granoo and Daddy to cut the leaves, what say? And then . . . we can have pizzas later!'

Tara went to bed happy, thinking about her costume.

Shweta left Tara's room, rubbing her temples. She had a headache . . . and a heartache. She recalled how she had married Vikram despite her parents' objections.

'How can you fall in love with him? He is as black as the night with no moon. We won't even spot him if there is a power cut!' Her mom had said. Over time, things did get better, but when Tara was born, Shweta knew that her daughter's skin colour had disappointed her mother. But for her mother to tell the child this? It was unimaginable!

Shweta had to wait till Vikram came home to vent her anger. 'It's amazing. Things have not changed at all! The same old plays about princesses and the same old attitudes. When will we stop judging people? Even my own mother! I was too fair, and now Taru is too dark. I can't talk to Ma. I'll yell. Should we talk to Sangeeta Miss?'

'If you feel Taru is happy about being the magical tree, let it be for now. She will do her best. And we can gently talk to Ma one of these days. But I am amazed that the teacher said such a thing, though. How do we deal with this, I wonder.'

Shweta really didn't have the answer. She felt she had walked through a looking glass and gone over to the other side. The same looking glass that had been her companion all her life, lay shattered today in more pieces than she had thought possible. Each broken reflection staring back at her told her a different story. Each story, however ugly, was honest and truthful.

She knew what she had to do. Shweta messaged Malini. 'I'll attend the alumni bash. Tell Madhavi to send me a formal invite and the details.'

♡♡

Shweta received the Vidya Niketan Achiever Award amidst thunderous applause. She got off the stage and went straight to her family.

'So proud of you,' Vikram whispered in her ear. Tara enveloped her in a big hug. Shweta placed her award on the table, kissed Tara and said, 'I'll be right back.'

She walked with a thudding heart and a determined step towards the table where the gang of four were seated. It was time to blend the broken reflections into a whole. It was time to break the colour bar.

MY MANE CONCERN

Ratna Manucha

It was the autumn of 2019, a few months short of the deadly attack by the dreaded C. No, not cancer, because that is the first word that comes to mind, but Covid, a freshly coined word—one that nobody had ever heard of before. In the coming months, people's lives all over the world would turn upside down. Closer home, here in India, Ramona's world, too, was about to turn topsy-turvy, but for a different reason.

Like trees in autumn, Ramona's hair was shedding. Every morning, Ramona would wake up to a fresh fall. A large clump on her pillow, like a cluster of ominous black spiders with sprawled legs, ungainly clumps in the bathroom drain . . . hair . . . hair everywhere. And it was not just at night-time. It was all over the floors of her house even during the day. Anytime and every time she touched her hair, a bunch came out in her hand.

One morning, she parted her hair and stood in front of the mirror, staring in stunned horror. There was a shiny, round spot on her scalp. This couldn't be happening! Not to her! She, who was known in her class for her beautiful, healthy mane! How could she face her friends now? Oh, the shame. The ignominy of it all! But there was no time to think or brood. The CLAT exams were knocking at her door. She wanted to pursue law as a career, and the Common Law Admission Test was the first step towards it. Besides, the board exams were also just around the corner.

'Maybe it's the weather,' she thought distractedly. 'I'll just wear a cap to school till I figure out what to do. I'll deal with it after the CLAT exams.' She had a vague idea that hair fall occurred during certain seasons; she just couldn't remember when.

The cap idea was a complete flop. It was too warm, and she attracted sniggers and cocky questions to which she had no answers.

'The sky falling on your head, Chicken Little?'

'It's about to snow, eh?'

Ramona wanted to curl up in a corner and die. The cap was discarded.

'I think I'll talk to Mummy this weekend,' she mumbled to herself as she tried to cover up the bald patch by tying up her hair in an untidy top knot.

The weekend came and went. Ramona's mother had to meet some clients at work, so she left early morning and came back late at night on both days. Both times, by the time she was back, Ramona was asleep in bed.

Ramona's mother was dealing with struggles of her own. She had started a new job, and a lot of her time and energy were spent in trying to placate her unreasonable new boss.

The days passed. The weather changed, and winter arrived. The first hazy rays of the early morning sun were trying desperately to break through the winter smog. Yet the autumn in Ramona's life remained steadfast. Another bald patch had shown up. Ramona was mortified. Alarm bells went off in her head. What followed was endless nights of crying forlornly into her pillow and going to school all bleary-eyed in the morning.

What was wrong with her? How serious was this issue with her hair? Would there be more bald patches? Or (heaven forbid!) was this a harbinger of worse things to come? Was she going to die? These questions kept churning round and round in her head, like a noisy mixer that wouldn't stop because she just could not figure out how to press the 'stop' button.

Should she message her father? But he was sailing and was so far away. He would feel helpless, and it would only upset him. No, she had to get hold of her mother, somehow.

By now, Ramona had begun noticing the strange looks directed towards her by her classmates. 'What is with this unruly hairstyle?' they seemed to be asking her. The questioning looks were beginning to alarm Ramona. Nobody questioned her directly, not even her best friend. And Ramona herself was too confused to broach the topic with her friends. Would they understand her fears? Or would they laugh at her? After all, there had been so many times when they had all ganged up to tease and snigger at some of their classmates for trivial and silly matters. She, too, had been a part of the gang. So, what would stop them from doing the same to her now?

On three or four occasions, the class teacher punished Ramona for disobedience. She felt Ramona had not listened to her when she asked her to comb her hair properly. Missing school was out of the question, but each morning, Ramona woke up with a sick feeling in the pit of her stomach. Her concentration went haywire as her mind was constantly wandering back to her patchy pate.

'Mummy, we need to talk urgently,' Ramona texted her mother one morning on her way to school. But as usual, her mother had left early for work even though it was a Saturday. That evening, though, she returned home earlier than usual; she had never received such a message from her daughter in all these years.

'What happened, my darling?'

As soon as she heard the concern in her mother's voice, Ramona broke down. Bitter tears coursed down her cheeks as she parted her hair to show her mother the two shining bald patches on her head.

'How long has this been going on?' Ramona's mother asked with a worried frown, crinkling her forehead.

'Almost a month and a half,' blubbered Ramona.

'And you took this long to tell me? You do know that we live in the same house, don't you?'

Ramona opened her mouth to respond to her mother's sarcastic comment, but then shut it again. From past experience, she knew that once the mother-daughter team got embroiled in a war of words, there was no stopping them.

On her part, Ramona's mother was mortified when she thought of the many occasions when she had seen the floor of the house littered with fallen hair and had brushed any concerns she may have had under the carpet—literally. There was too much on her plate, being a single working mother for the better part of the year.

'Chop, chop. Get up, and stop looking so gloomy,' said her mother briskly as she got up to look for her phone. 'I'm on the job now. You'll be right as rain in no time. Let me fix up an appointment with a dermatologist.'

And so it began—the endless rounds from one doctor to another. One thing was clear. The hair loss that Ramona was witnessing was not due to a change in season. It now had a name, albeit a tongue-twisting name. Still, a name nonetheless: *alopecia areata.*

'Trust my ailment to have such an unpronounceable name,' she muttered to herself.

They finally settled on Dr Prasad, a balding, middle-aged man with kind, twinkling eyes behind round, rimless glasses.

'I wonder if he has the same problem as me,' Ramona found her mind wandering as she stared idly at his receding hairline. 'If he hasn't been able to cure himself, how on earth is he going to cure me?'

But the doctor's voice jerked her back to the present, and she began listening to him earnestly.

'Alopecia is a condition of sudden hair loss that starts with one or more bald patches in the scalp. It is an auto-immune disease. Which means the cells in one's immune system surround and attack the hair follicles. We will start with some ointments and multivitamins and see how she responds.' Dr Prasad smiled genially as he got up to pat Ramona on the back.

'See? That wasn't so bad, was it?' Ramona's mother cocked an eyebrow at her as they headed back home, armed with four different tubes of ointments in varying sizes.

Ramona applied the ointments diligently, thrice a day. She had to go into the washroom during recess to apply one of the ointments. Her classmates soon understood that her going to the washroom at the exact same time each day meant something serious. After all, she couldn't be wanting to pee every day at the same time, now, could she?

It was time she was confronted. The task fell upon two of Ramona's closest friends, Asit and Tara. They accosted her after school that Saturday, just as she was about to walk out of the gate.

'What's up?' Ramona said nonchalantly, trying hard to still her rapidly beating heart when she found them blocking her way and looking at her rather grimly. Deep within her, she knew what was coming next.

'Don't you think you need to tell us something?' asked Tara, worry writ large on her face.

'C'mon, confess!' added Asit. His tone surprised Ramona. He sounded genuinely concerned.

Hearing the concern of her friends and seeing their eyes crinkle in worry, Ramona felt as if a heavy load had been lifted off her chest. They certainly didn't look as though they were going to laugh at her. A dry sob escaped from her as tears began welling up in her eyes. Tara hugged her wordlessly. Something was not quite right.

Ramona pulled them towards a corner of the rapidly emptying school ground. There was no holding back now—the days of self-doubt, the endless trips to doctors and, so far, no solution in sight. The floodgates opened, and Ramona sobbed her heart out. It was such a relief to be able to confide in her friends, her soulmates.

'It's not how other people see you,' said Asit as he hugged her. 'It's how you see yourself. Just change your attitude towards yourself, and you will begin to see things differently.'

'After all, there's more to you to love than just your hair,' added Tara helpfully and threw her arms around Ramona.

Nearly giddy with relief, Ramona hugged both her friends hard.

School did not seem like such an ordeal after this. The smile on her face returned. Her classmates and teachers now knew about her condition. Nobody gave her pitying looks. They treated her the way they had done earlier. Such a relief! Now that her secret was out of the way, she got down to studying earnestly. Many times, during classes, her top knot would open up to reveal the two bald patches, but she would just roll her hair back into the unruly bun that she had grown accustomed to.

The ointments had proved quite ineffective. However, the next visit to Dr Prasad gave her a glimmer of hope. He wanted to start injecting some steroids into the bald patches.

'I cannot promise anything, but this would be our last try. I would like to give this a shot.'

Ramona smiled at the pun, glad that her sense of humour was still intact.

'You will have to come to my clinic once a month for the next six months. If the hair has to grow again, we will know by then,' Dr Prasad concluded.

The pricks were painful, to put it mildly. The pain coursed through her head, bringing tears to her eyes. Sometimes, the scalp would bleed where the needle had pricked. But Ramona gritted her teeth and held on.

'I've got to see this through,' she would tell herself repeatedly.

Spring sprung. The seeds that had been planted earlier began to sprout tender, fresh and green leaves. Nature's bounty abounded, but an uneasy calm pervaded the atmosphere. Ominous virus clouds had begun to gather everywhere, and the shrill sounds of ambulance sirens were echoing eerily through the air every few minutes. Covid, the pandemic, had reared its ugly head, and working from home became the new norm. Classes all over the world were now being conducted online. It was most disconcerting.

In Ramona's world, the season hadn't changed. Her bald patches were as barren as the tundra. She checked her scalp two to three times a day but could not spot any tiny hair growing. She even tried inspecting her head using a magnifying glass. Standing in front of the mirror with her hand guiding the apparatus, she studied the reflection of her scalp but could spot nothing. Nope. *Nada. Niets.* By now, the doctor's consultation was also conducted online. The prognosis was bleak.

'I don't want you to follow any more treatments,' the good doctor told Ramona, kindly. 'I suggest we wait and watch. Let's be patient. We've done all we could. The hair might grow back. In any case, I think we have halted further hair loss.'

Doctor Prasad had passed his verdict. Ramona was in a daze. She vaguely remembered her mother's arm around her shoulders after the Zoom call finished. No more injections, no more ointments, no more hope.

The next few days passed in a blur. Her tears seemed to have dried up. After a week of despondently slouching around the house, looking as miserable as she felt, Ramona woke up one morning with a sudden feeling that she finally knew how to press the 'stop' button for the thoughts in her head. After all, she was the loved and adored daughter of a hard-working mother who thought the sun rose and set with her. There was nothing to do, she told herself. There really wasn't. For her mother's sake, it was high time she got on with her life.

'If you can't beat 'em, join 'em!' she told herself. Clearly, moping around or being anxious was not helping. The doctor had also told Ramona and her mother that she needed to de-stress. Stress could make the alopecia restart. She couldn't deal with that.

'I know what I want for my birthday,' she announced two weeks later as she flopped on her bed, her untidy locks framing her face.

'What?' asked her mother without looking up from her laptop.

'A new hairstyle! Mom, ask your hairdresser if he can come home and cut my hair real short and style it in such a way that the bald patches get covered. I need to stop thinking about what is missing and start focusing on what I have. In fact, I can see endless possibilities in front of me. How about if I shave my head? That would look real cool, too!'

Her mother stopped punching the keyboard and looked up. She stared at her daughter wordlessly.

Ramona went on, 'I need to get on with my life. I've spent far too much time brooding over my bald patches. It's time I accepted them as a part of me. You see, Mum, when one finds no solution to a problem, it's probably not a problem to be solved but rather a truth to be accepted. After all, the word 'imperfect' can be changed by just adding an apostrophe: I'm perfect!'

Ramona's mother stared at her daughter admiringly. Ramona grinned as her mother rose, held up her index and middle finger to form a V-for-victory sign and walked towards her phone to make an appointment with the hairdresser.

RAW

Janani Balaji

There are days when my fingers reach, over and over and over, these little stubs of anxiety, pulling stars out of a blotchy red constellation of shame on my face. The skin is raw, and my fingertips are cast in metal. I get yelled at for having blood on my face. I scratch it again.

It's Pavlovian, in a sense. This urge. It is like my body's response to coffee in the morning. It's the indulgence of insanity where my hands are covered with little white scars, criss-crossing in a mesh that once cradled my fall. But now it suffocates me. My skin is raw, my face is bleeding, and my nails have skin under them as I gnaw them off. I am a pitiful person.

I look into the mirror and only see signs of struggle but no signs of victory. I have never worn shorts that go above my knees. I desperately will my heart to stop, but it keeps going. Life keeps going. I keep going.

I pluck an apple and crush it in my palm. The juices trickle down my hand, down my arm and down my chest. I am sticky with guilt. A snake laps it up. It whispers to me, tells me secrets in a language I cannot understand, but I greedily consume it all, just in case. There are reasons why I have been cast out, and it knows them all. It knows the curve of my heart; the hair on my thighs that tangle with the flick of my wrist.

My father tells me to wax. I wonder why that is his only concern with my skin. I wonder why he is only concerned with my skin.

I am a product of my mind—my thoughts, my dreams that I crushed underfoot a flood of my own tears. My ice-cold heart slumbers, and I shiver.

In school, I watch people smile from my corner, the farthest corner in class. It is too loud here. I want to plug my ears, but my fingers only reach up to itch-itch-itch under my chin, on my neck, on my chest. Nobody notices. I scratch more—a subconscious need to placate myself. I must deal with my problems on my own.

Is this what you wanted?

My shoulders are a mess of pus-filled craters, dried blood and nail marks. I did not do well in my tests.

I swallow a pill I am not allowed to know the name of. My jaw clicks because it was opened too wide. I am open too wide, yet I cannot find air to breathe. My skin grows messier still.

I cannot face mirrors; I cannot face myself. I know this, and I weep. And I keep weeping till my eyes are puffy, underlined with my sleepless nights. I dare not touch my skin or I might tear it off. I can't stand it. It's uncomfortable. I'm uncomfortable. I want out—out of my skin, my mind, this curse that I've cast upon myself.

I scream. I drink water and pick at my skin again.

Imperfect body, imperfect mind. I cannot stand the inside or the outside. The core is rotten, and the apple is covered in mould. But when did it start to rot?

Scorn and disdain and pity and snickers and snickers and snickers about everything. A little limp, I stagger towards hope. The sun rips the light from the flesh to reveal the void, and I am alone. I am all alone.

I don't like thinking. I pick at my skin again. I pick and push and rub at my acrid skin, blossoming with red. Unbridled fury swirls beneath. My stubby, chewed-off nails are sore with the skin I bit off my finger pads—I am incapable of control.

When night falls, I trace my fingers over the jagged flesh. It braces, pushing up against me. I push myself down, heavy and lead filled. My bones are heavy, I lie. I am heavy. My body inflates with curves I never wanted. My shirts grow tight, and I lose my once-familiar sense of self. I am mature for my age; I feel like a child. I am lost and scared and alone. I wish I could just go home.

Home is any place where I'm not in this skin. My skin that strains and constricts and coils around me. It contorts my heart.

I can hear the smell of incense and taste the ringing of my mother's altar bell. My brain is on wrong today too, so I plug my ears and lie face down on the floor. I don't even have the energy to pick my skin today. The redness fades a little. My eyes well with tears, but I am too tired to cry or say anything. I simply lie on the floor, face down, and let gravity do the work. Nobody is proud of the wretched wreck I am.

My father knocks on the door.

'Are you working? You should be working. Why aren't you working?' The questions pour in fast and quick. I don't open the door.

The scale sits heavy in my room, and as I look at it, I imagine smashing it against the wall over and over until it shatters, and all that's left of the wretched thing is the glass shards in my hands. I take a moment to breathe. I pull down the sleeves of my shirt, pull them down so I can't see my arms; can't pick at what you can't see, right? Out of sight, out of mind. Out of mind. I'm going out of my mind.

I click my pen and do my homework. I find a derivative, use the cosine rule, draw a triangle and write a proof. My science textbook tells me no lies. Unlike me. When the sun rises again, I will be alright. I will be alright when it counts. As far as we need to know, I am alright.

I raise the night to my lips and swallow it whole. For a moment, I feel like God, then crumble to bits.

The map of my skin carries ridges, bumps and valleys, inflamed and red, crying over the little white scars from when I caved.

I am struggle itself, but I am alive.

♡♡

Acne is a common cause of stress among teens. But when acne is combined with bad self-image issues and anxiety, it triggers skin picking as a way to relieve stress. When it becomes frequent and intense, it turns into a skin-picking disorder or excoriation. It leaves the skin red and raw and an out-of-control case of acne that requires therapy and medication. This story is an attempt to raise awareness on an issue that can be a scream for help.

LIFE IN THE HEADLINES

Nandini Nayar

The whispers begin the minute she walks in through the gates of her new school. *No surprises there*, Shalu thinks. This is how she was welcomed at the six other schools before this one.

She crosses the gravel path and starts climbing the stairs leading to the main door of the building. Now, nudges are being exchanged, heads are turning as she walks down the corridor. Little explosions of laughter come to her ears. She sees eyes widen and jaws drop. Don't they know that their faces give them away? These eyes-widened, jaw-dropping-in-surprise people—surely, they aren't that dumb? She passes groups of boys and girls, giggling, sudden snorts of laughter bursting out of them. Why, it's almost as if there's a huge newspaper-style headline hovering over their heads, in bold letters, that says: **It's an elephant; it's a hippo . . . no, it's a new girl!**

Headlines are meant to be read, which is why they are in those thick, dark letters. And that's why no one tries to hide them. No one attempts to make them smaller . . . or less hurtful. Except at home, of course, where Amma is constantly scanning the things people say and do so that she can stop the ugly words from reaching Shalu's ears, so that she can save her from the hurt. It's like there's a constant headline over Amma's head, too. At times, it says: **Keep it from Shalu!** At other times, it says: **What not to talk about to Shalu.**

Shalu knows that Amma has two lists running through her head. One is a list of the things that she can tell her daughter. This one has silly, everyday things that aren't likely to upset Shalu. On this list is also anything to do with school, studies, exams and higher education. There's a certain logic that's at work here, and after years of observing the grown-ups around her, Shalu now knows what that logic is.

Amma (and the world with her) thinks fat girls ≠ love life. And so, Amma (and the world with her) decide, fat girls = studies + books + interest in academics.

The other list of Amma's has things that she tells Baba when Shalu isn't around. On it are stories about girls who do the kinds of things that teenagers are supposed to do—partying with hordes of friends and spending the rest of the time talking to them on the phone. Exciting tales of ongoing battles with their parents about the clothes they buy and the things they do also feature here. Amma's friends and cousins and colleagues supply her with these stories, and she laps up the details and then pours them out to Baba when he's trying to read the newspaper.

Amma says none of this to Shalu, who has moved schools too often to have friends. And who, therefore, has no one to chat or go to parties with. And she says nothing at all about the boyfriends these girls begin to acquire and the ecstasy and heartache they bring. She's doing it to protect Shalu, but surely, she can't think her daughter is blind and stupid. After all, Shalu spends all day with boys and girls. Normal boys and normal girls. She sees the way they look at each other, eyes sliding casually before they stop at the face that's taken their fancy. Sometimes, the eyes catch and hold, and Shalu knows then that there'll be a new couple in the class in a few days. Those same eyes slide over her when she walks into her new classroom. But once they've taken in her size, they widen and jump, as if she's the obstacle they want to avoid. And instantly, headlines appear over their heads: **Is that the new girl? How much does she weigh?**

The boys are turning away, their shoulders shaking as they laugh into their cupped hands. They slap each other's backs on the new joke that's walked into their lives. The girls stare at her, seeing the way the school skirt bulges out under the belt in the front and back. The uniform looks like a sack tied around her middle. They manage to see everything in that one sweep—the thickness of Shalu's legs, the wobbly bits that hang from her arms and jiggle with every movement. They are glad to see all this. Shalu can see it in the words dancing over their heads: **That's not me! I am thinner than her!**

They exchange glances, congratulating each other, celebrating their thinness, their extraordinary normalness. It takes them a minute more to realize what Shalu's entry means, and when it does, Shalu sees the horrified headline that appears over them: **Who will sit beside her?**

There are desperate whispers and the girls who sit by themselves get the sympathy of the rest of the class. But sympathy is overrated when it doesn't offer any solutions. Shalu has come up with various headlines that describe their situation. The two best ones are: **Ten ways to avoid sitting next to the new girl** and **how to get out of sharing a desk with the fat, new girl.**

And when the class teacher, Mrs Rajan, asks, 'Who will sit beside Shalu and be her friend', all their clever plans come into play. Some of them become immersed in their books; others gaze into the distance. Shalu has seen these expressions several times and knows exactly what headlines go with each: **Hardworking students at work; dreams of the future in their eyes.**

But none of these tricks had worked in any of the six schools Shalu had been to so far, and they don't work here either.

'Nimmy,' Mrs Rajan calls out, and a sigh of relief rustles around the room. Everyone, except the unfortunate Nimmy, relaxes. Nimmy scoots to one end of the seat, her bag held protectively in front of her. Relax, Shalu wants to tell her, fatness isn't catching. Stupidity sometimes is, but Nimmy gives her no chance to find out if she's stupid or not. She sits rigidly turned away, carefully keeping to her side of the desk. Shalu doesn't mind. She knows the bitter thoughts going through the girl's head right now.

Why me? Always unlucky! This is what Nimmy of Class 11 C is probably thinking.

Shalu settles down at her desk, glad she's no longer in front of the room with all those eyes on her. Of course, people are still turning in their seats to look at her, as if they can't believe someone this different is sitting with them. Mrs Rajan notices this but allows her eyes to slip and slide away. Shalu is familiar with this routine because she's seen many grown-ups do it. They see children call her mean names or make loud, rude jokes at her expense, but instead of stopping them, they let their eyes slip and slide away. Grown-ups, Shalu has learnt, are the most undependable people in the world.

She looks at the timetable she's copied from the uncooperative Nimmy, who slid over her diary reluctantly and then snatched it away. It's maths next. Shalu cheers up because she likes the subject. She likes that six and eight have rounded bits that stick out, just like she does. She likes that the numbers keep the others in her class busy, so no one has the time to come up with jokes about her. Perhaps it's because of this that Shalu has become pretty good at maths. The most difficult of problems and equations come magically untangled for her. Shalu wishes that other magical things would happen in maths class, too. That the boy at the front of the class would turn in his seat and look at her. Smile at her maybe. But, of course, that's not the kind of magic even numbers can help her with. So, she settles down to solving the problems Mr Nath is explaining. Then, halfway through, the magical peace of a maths class is broken.

'And how do we calculate the weight of a really fat person?' someone asks, and a wave of giggles breaks out. Shalu feels all eyes turn to her. There's a moment of dismay that she hasn't seen this coming because she's been left adrift, without any headlines to help her. Her headlines help carve out a distance between her and the joke, making the whole episode seem like it is happening to someone else.

'Don't be silly,' the maths teacher scolds, his eyes doing the slip and slide routine, and leaping over Shalu in the third row.

'And what about a small brain?' someone asks at that moment and there's an immediate shift in the focus of the class. Shalu wonders who the new target is. One quick look around the room and she sees what Mr Nath has chosen to slide over. The class is throwing amused looks at a boy in front of her. Shalu can see the back of his head, large and lumpy. The lumps seem like a silly reason to tease someone. But when it comes to laughing at others, Shalu knows that the silliest excuse will do.

The boy with the lumpy head is constantly in trouble. His name is Mandeep, and Mr Nath calls out to him again and again, asking him questions, getting him to work out problems. The questions fluster Mandeep, and he stammers as he tries to answer. But his answers are never right, and they set off fresh waves of giggles. By the end of the class, Mandeep is slumped in his seat, and his notebook is filled with savage red marks.

Will he ever learn? The boy who failed maths! Shalu has seen enough children like Mandeep to guess that these are the kinds of headlines floating in the minds of her classmates. They walk out for the break, laughing and chatting, glad they are not different, glad they are not meant for failure.

Shalu stares at the lumps on Mandeep's head till, eventually, Mandeep feels her eyes on him and turns around. There's surprise written on his face, but there is also something that resembles a grateful misery. There's a grading, even among those who don't fit, and Shalu knows that in this rock-paper-scissors world, she is at the bottom of the list. The very-skinny, the too-tall, the not-good-enough, the stutterers, all triumph over the fat, the obese, the too-large. And so, before Mandeep can say anything, she says, 'I think you need help with maths. I can help you.'

Maths is fun, but it can get tiring, especially when you are trying to get someone like Mandeep to understand how it works. He is so deeply convinced he's terrible with numbers that it takes ages for Shalu to get him to look past that thought. And now, she's ready for a little rest. She knows that she'll get it in games class because she knows exactly what will happen there. The teacher will throw them a ball, pick two captains and ask them to select their teams. She knows the battle that's coming and even has the headlines ready in her head: **Who will have the fat new girl? Captains battle it out over new girl!**

Of course, neither captain will choose her. And that will leave her free to find a shady tree to relax under. Today, the arguments take a little longer, and Shalu stands alone, waiting to get away.

'I pick the new girl,' a tall girl with long plaits says. Shalu has heard the others call her Atiya and thinks how well the name suits her. She's mildly surprised that Atiya wants her on the team.

'That's not fair,' the other captain calls.

'What's not fair?' tall Atiya demands.

Then Niharika, the other captain, says, 'You are getting two people, because she's so big!' The students burst into laughter. Shalu walks towards a tree that has a large platform built around it. Being fat means constantly being surprised by the meanness of people's thoughts. Being fat means making jokes about yourself and then laughing at them before anyone else can. If you don't, you find yourself all alone. Shalu doesn't mind the aloneness. She's used to being a group of one.

But today, she is not alone under the tree. There's a boy there. He looks up from the book he's reading to ask, 'So, they kicked you out, too?' And without waiting for her answer, he goes back to his book. Shalu has no time to feel sorry for herself because she's so busy wondering why this boy, who is not too thin or too fat, doesn't stammer or smell funny, has been left out of the teams. Headline after headline chase each other: **Mystery shrouds boy's rejection from team. Why was he left out?**

Then, a sharp whistle sounds, and he looks up. 'End of freedom,' he says with a sigh and slides off the platform. He stumbles, and Shalu sees that his right foot is twisted. She should have helped him down. To make up for it, she walks behind him, ready to grab him if he needs help.

'See you in the next games period,' he says and limps away. His name, she discovers, is Siddhant. He spends every games period on that platform under the tree. He always has a book and, after the first 'Hello', says nothing till the bell rings. It is oddly comforting to sit on the platform in silence and Shalu enjoys the time very much indeed. When the bell rings, she hurriedly leaps off the platform and stands there, ready to help Siddhant if he stumbles again. He does stumble sometimes, but for all her determination to help him, she never does anything. She has a feeling that he wouldn't like it if she did, and so she merely keeps an alert watch over him till he is safely back in his seat.

Perhaps their time spent together under the tree is making some difference, for Siddhant never joins in the laughter that breaks out when someone teases her. And, of course, there's always someone finding something new to tease her about. Shalu isn't surprised because that's how it has always been at every school she's attended. When she climbs into the school bus, people scream and pretend the bus is tilting. When she's asked to solve maths problems on the blackboard, she hears the laughs and feels the stares pierce her back. And when it's time for the medical examination, her experience has taught Shalu what to expect. People want to know how much she weighs. In the corridors, she hears people making guesses and placing bets. And the minute the nurse calls out her weight, it's all over the school: 'New girl weighs record-breaking ninety kgs!' The girl who broke the weighing machine.

At one of Shalu's previous schools, there was a nurse who refused to tell anyone how much she weighed. Shalu still remembers the surprised gratitude she had felt and how gladly she had agreed to stay back when the nurse asked her to. She was preparing to thank the nurse and tell her how kind she had been. But before she could utter a word, the nurse leaned in and said, 'You are grossly overweight! You know, don't you?'

Shalu was startled. She felt thick dread fill her stomach and wanted to escape, but the nurse held her captive with an angry grip on her arm. All Shalu could do was nod. Yes, she was (still is) overweight. And surprise, surprise, she did know it.

'Then do something about it,' the nurse had hissed in rage, throwing Shalu's arm away, as if it disgusted her. 'Just stop stuffing yourself!'

Shalu still remembers the shock and hurt she felt then. Did the nurse really think she was fat because she ate too much? Since then, Shalu has discovered that most people do believe that. At school, every time she opens her lunch box, people lean over their desks to peer in. They seem surprised at the normal-sized box and even more surprised to see the two rotis in it. Shalu puts up with their jokes and comments because she dreads what is coming.

Soon, it will be school day. Shalu watches her classmates being selected for various events. She sees the teachers eye her, mentally measuring her up and trying to fit her somewhere. Each time they look at her, Shalu reads various exasperated headlines in their eyes: **What shall we do with her? The girl who did not fit any role!**

Shalu is happy to watch the others dance, sing and practise their lines. She has Siddhant for company, reading a book as always. Then there's Mandeep, determinedly battling maths problems.

Besides them, there are three girls who are also sitting at their desks. They aren't in any dance or even the play, and so, they stay where they are, scattered like islands around the classroom. The participants are very busy at the front of the room. Soon, the actors and the dancers need more space, so desks are pushed aside with large screeches, and the non-participants find themselves scrunched together in a corner of the classroom. The three girls, Jasmine, Sujana and Sania, are neither fat nor do they limp. And their heads seem pretty normal. Shalu feels new headlines flutter to life: **What was their fault? Why did they not click?**

'I . . . I kh . . . khant s . . . sp . . . speak pro . . . properly!' Jasmine explains.

'Too dark,' Sujana says. Beside her, Sania giggles, 'We'll need too much make-up to be seen!' She's perfected the art of making jokes at herself and has learnt how to use them, so no one ever knows how much the colour of her skin actually matters.

Shalu thinks she can guess, but it's not an exact science, this peering into the thoughts that rush through a person's mind. There's a headline glowing in Shalu's head, filling her with relief: **Not alone! Misfits of the class!**

Not for long, Shalu tells herself stoutly. Just a few days more, and then school day will be in the past, and they can forget about it for another year. And once the dancers and actors take off their fancy clothes and make-up, they stop being grown-up and glamourous strangers. They are once again students of 11 C and relieved headlines dance through Shalu's head: **Back to the routine! Return of the normal!**

And now Shalu thinks she can feel at home here. She's no longer the new girl. What's more, she has a few people to share smiles with. She has learnt to gauge where danger lies and prepare for it. Perhaps this lulls her into a feeling of security when she should know that her size will always make her a victim.

That's how Shalu discovers that language, too, can be a weapon. It's the English period, and Mrs Rajan has just finished teaching them a poem. They are now discussing similes and metaphors and hyperboles and ready to make their own figures of speech.

'As big as an elephant,' is the first one.

'As large as a circus tent,' someone says and giggles.

'She was an elephant in the room,' is offered as an example of a metaphor.

'She was so fat that she could be seen from space,' is a hyperbole that unleashes giggles.

'She was so fat that she was given a separate pin code,' is the next one.

As laughter erupts in the classroom, Shalu feels her classmates' eyes on her and is furious with herself. Why did she think she would be safe in the English class? She is hurt because she has allowed herself to feel safe. It will not happen again because she will take care to be prepared.

Meanwhile, her classmates are discovering exactly how effective figures of speech can be. By the time Mrs Rajan understands what's going on and puts an end to it, the damage is done. Shalu has learnt the dangers that litter the English class and thought up headlines to describe her feelings: **Words that hurt! These words bite; they sting.**

In the days that follow, Shalu stays alert in English classes. Mrs Rajan has moved on to the next lesson. But who knows what dangers lie ahead? And when Mrs Rajan announces, 'Today we are going to learn how to write headlines,' Shalu knows she's been right to stay alert. Headlines are short and snappy; they compress so many things in them. They have lessons from past experiences and forecasts for the future, and they have helped her make sense of things that happen around her. But the others? What will they do with a headline? In their clumsy paws, this will be a new game, a weapon to prod her into pain.

'Write a headline to describe someone,' Mrs Rajan instructs them.

Shalu stares at the teacher in horror. How can she be so blind? Does she not see what she's doing? Heart thumping, she bends over her notebook and waits to see what will happen next.

'Ready to read out your headlines?' Mrs Rajan asks.

Of course they are! Hands wave frantically, trying to attract the teacher's attention. The air is full of begging calls of, 'Miss, Miss!'

'Fat girl thumps the ground, tilts the earth,' is the first one. Giggles erupt, but today, Mrs Rajan doesn't play blind. 'Don't write nonsense,' she snaps.

So, the next few are careful insults, worded so they won't get the speakers into trouble.

'Do overweight children cause starvation?' is one.

'Do fat children grow into fat adults?' comes next.

Never, Shalu thinks mournfully, will she enjoy an English class again. She will always be too on edge, too alert to possible insults.

'Shalu,' someone says, and she jerks around. It is Siddhant. 'Shalu—being human to the boy who limps!'

Now Jasmine stands up to say, 'The G . . . girl w . . . who understands m . . . my w . . . wh . . . whords!'

'Friendship means looking past the skin!' Sujana adds.

'The girl who can always cheer you up!' Sania calls out.

And now people are turning around in their seats to look at Shalu. But this is a different kind of looking. This is a coming awake kind of a surprise, as if they are seeing her for the first time. As if the headlines have introduced Shalu to them for the first time and they are ready to give her a chance.

She sees surprise on some faces and laughter on others. She's not won any battle, she knows. And it's not over yet. It probably never will be. But at least today, in the English class of the seventh school she has attended, Shalu has seen a beginning. It's tiny, and it looks like it could collapse in the next few minutes. But for now, it fills Shalu with hope and a brand-new headline that unfolds in her mind: **Can fat girls dream?**

THE MOST BEAUTIFUL GIRL IN THE WORLD

Priyanka Sinha Jha

'Mirror, mirror on the wall. Who's the prettiest of us all?' whispered Asha as she turned around to face the mirror.

She stared at herself in the mirror and sighed, 'Nope, that didn't work. I still resemble one of those ugly wooden masks sold on Janpath.' Then, carefully adjusting her hair to the left side of her face, Asha attempted to blink with her right eye. No movement. None whatsoever. The eyelid refused to budge even a millimetre, the right eye glaring back at her, wide open in a ceaseless stare, while the left eyelid drooped like a wilting lily.

Exasperated, she now tried putting on a cute goofball smile and tried to accentuate it with just a dab of lipstick, but her lips, in sheer defiance, pulled in the other direction of her semi-paralysed face.

Asha opened up the cupboard and pulled out the 'dress'. The elegant moss green one from Zara. The dress she had been admiring in the display window of the flagship store for the longest time. The dress that her parents had promised to get her for a 'very special occasion'. And then, finally, the occasion arrived. The school farewell party for tenth-grade students ready to step out into the world of grown-ups. Her parents, thrilled at the news that Asha had decided to go to her school party, had bought the dress as a special gift. But the elegant knee-length dress did not transform Asha into a stunning young lady as she'd hoped. It just made her look like a Janpath wooden-mask-face person in a green dress.

Just then, to Asha's utter relief, her friend Tanya glided into the room.

'Hey girl!' she trilled.

'Hey, Tans. I am getting cold feet about going to the school farewell party. I know it was my own bright idea, but now it feels kind of super scary.'

Tanya stole a quick look at Asha's image in the mirror before plonking down on the bed.

'Why? What's wrong?' she asked.

'Dude, can't you see? I look like a freak with these weird eyes and drooling lips! If I go to the party, Zara may sue me for making their dress look bad in public.'

'Then, you could pretend it's a fancy-dress party and totally go as a stylish zombie,' Tanya shot back jokingly.

Asha burst out laughing.

Tanya knew better than to offer her friend any pity; Asha hated that. Although Asha seemed to have taken her disfigurement after a recent accident quite sportingly, Tanya knew that Asha, her childhood 'chaddi-buddy', was covering up her emotions and trying to be the strong, cool type of gal. The only way to help was to find some humour in the situation. Laughter was the best medicine at this point in time.

Although she was a good student, Asha had always longed to be beautiful and slim. Being a chubby kid with a voracious appetite, she was often teased about being tubby. Asha hated the teasing and the nicknames . . . Chubs . . . Roly-Poly . . . so many others. Despite Mummy's reassurances that it was all just puppy fat and would go away once she grew up, Asha was not so sure that her fat would magically disappear. But, when her teen years arrived, the fat did indeed pare itself down. But like all teenagers, Asha was still unsatisfied. She was eagerly waiting for the gawky ugly-duckling phase to end and for her transformation into the proverbial swan to begin. Although the wait seemed unending, appreciative second glances from the boys in school had begun coming her way, making Asha feel optimistic about her prospects in life.

It was at this significant juncture that the dreadful accident took place.

Dadi was convinced that it was their envious relatives who had brought this fate upon Asha. She was beside herself with worry about her granddaughter's looks 'getting spoilt'. After all, what good was education if a young girl didn't look good? It was certainly not adequate enough to land a suitable groom.

Papa was always wary of Asha's ability to handle herself in crowded places. Even though she was a teen, Papa would insist on holding Asha's hand and guiding her at the mall or the multiplex. Papa was sure that his little Asha had not been crazy enough to jump from a moving bus, but something had surely scared her. He blamed the crowds, the traffic, the state of the roads, and every other thing that he could think of for the mishap.

But Mummy had understood the real reason for Asha's accident. Mummy knew that Asha, in her obsession with losing weight, had been skipping her meals and epilepsy medication. Asha had concluded that the medications were preventing her from losing weight. It was Asha's mad obsession to lose weight fast that had caused her epileptic blackout and her consequent fall from the bus.

'This is why I have told you a thousand times to eat your breakfast before stepping out in the morning. I don't know what it is with you girls trying to be like thin wooden sticks,' scolded Mummy.

Asha had no clever counter. She knew it was true.

Asha had fallen while getting off a bus on the RK Puram Sector 12 Road, not very far from the tuition centre that she went to. The bus had taken off, and Asha was left lying unconscious on the road. If not for a vigilant ambulance driver who worked for a private hospital passing by that spot, she could have been lying unattended far longer and passed into a coma due to the concussion and internal bleeding in the head.

When her parents first saw her in the hospital, Asha was a jumble of tubes and wires, lying unconscious on a hospital bed.

Throughout her stay in the hospital, she was both drowsy and delirious in turns, courtesy of her medicines. Often, she woke up with her mouth as dry as paper, her lips pulling to one side and refusing to follow the usual pattern while eating. Adding to her woes was her eye, the right one. It had to be taped down with white cloth tape so that it did not get infected. There were no mirrors in the room or the attached bathroom, so she had never quite understood the full import of what had happened to her face. It was only after ten days, when she was finally in her senses that the doctor, Ashok Madaan, decided to break the news to her.

Doctor Madaan opened with, 'Beta, I want you to remember that this disfigurement is temporary, okay? At your age, full recovery will definitely happen sooner rather than later. The only thing you must be careful of is to avoid exposure to extremely cold temperatures. Wear a scarf on the head or wrap a muffler, okay?'

Asha nodded, not knowing where this conversation was headed. It was only when an attendant brought a mirror before her that the truth sank in. There she was, facing herself—her face twisted into a hideous mess. Asha was horrified. For the first time, Asha saw that she looked grotesque. Her eyes began to sting with tears.

She just covered her face with both hands and started sobbing inconsolably. Tears ran down her face. They flowed harder as she realized that her secret dream had perhaps been shattered. All of fifteen, the impressionable Asha had been secretly nursing the dream of grooming herself and becoming an international model.

It had all started with her devouring fashion magazines that featured gorgeous young women who looked like divine creatures. Their bodies and faces were sculpted to perfection, and their clothes fit with such precision that they appeared to have been fused with the body—not even a millimetre of bulge could be seen anywhere except in the right places.

Asha would cut out her own face from her photographs and stick it over the models' faces in the magazines, hoping that the universe would conspire to make her one, too.

Sixteen, Asha had learnt from the agency brochures, was the perfect age to become a model. So, in Asha's head, the time was just right. She was fifteen, with a year to spare.

Her childhood buddy Tanya was the only one who understood Asha's dream and helped her try to make it come true. With Tanya's help, Asha had secretly applied to Glam Up, a modelling agency that was holding a walk-in audition in a month's time. The only problem was that Asha's vital stats were far from desirable—a twenty-nine-inch waist—but she was working on it. In Asha's head, the countdown had begun. She had exactly thirty days to go for the audition, get selected and then a year, when she turned sixteen to start modelling professionally. After that, it would be 'Goodbye maths, science and history!'

In her preparation to qualify for the audition, Asha had been on a crash diet, starving herself in order to take that first step towards the dream. The minute she saw Asha skipping meals, Mummy knew she was up to something foolish. Between her multiple household chores and work at the office, Mummy tried her best to ensure that Asha was not starving herself. In fact, even Papa's help was enlisted, but somehow, Asha managed to find a way to diet and starve herself.

'Hai Bhagwan! Asha, if only you would pay as much attention to clearing the board exams, you would easily get ninety to ninety-five per cent,' Papa said to Asha as a mild rebuke. But all such rebukes and reprimands were water off a duck's back. Asha was convinced that she was grown up enough to know what was best for her. This was all a month before her accident.

In hindsight, Asha realized that her obsession with the audition had proved disastrous—the trifecta of not eating enough, sweltering Delhi heat and skipping her epilepsy medications had all combined and made her pass out at the most inopportune of moments.

Asha had been standing near the bus exit door as her stop was nearing, but she had blacked out and fallen off the bus.

Those moments before the blackout were still hazy, but it all began to come back to her during the days spent lying in the hospital bed.

The hospital stay finally ended when Asha was strong enough to move around on her own. In the first few weeks out of the hospital, Asha refused to attend school. Friends were sympathetic, helping her with class notes and assignments, and Tanya was her rock through this time. But Asha was happiest when she was in her room with photos of her favourite models on the mood board above the study table for company. But the models' faces seemed to be mocking her now. Their smiles seemed to hide a smirk, a smugness born from the knowledge that Asha would never stand among them.

Asha tried distracting herself as best as she could by burying her nose in schoolbooks, hoping her face would sort itself out soon.

Every morning, she would wake up and run to the mirror to check if there was even a flicker in her paralysed right eye. Sadly, the mirror was cruel—the sight it offered only made her weep, first a quiet whimper and then a loud howl that wracked her body. Later, she put on a brave face to face the world, quietly taping down her eyelid and forcing a smile before stepping out to greet her parents.

Two months went by, but there was no significant improvement in her condition. She sat alone in her room, scrolling through her photos on the phone. 'Will I ever look like my earlier self again?' Asha whispered to the smiling models on her wall. It seemed impossible. She had become 'Chubs' and 'Roly-Poly' all over again.

Dr Madaan, however, was ever hopeful and kept encouraging Asha to do all the normal things and not shut herself off like a recluse. It was just a matter of time, he kept telling her. Asha would have rolled her eyes, except that now she could not. Although the downward pull of her lip could easily be mistaken for her pulling a face.

Instead, she adopted a self-deprecating, humorous outlook to make herself feel better.

Despite all her attempts at jest and pretending as though things didn't affect her, inwardly, Asha was reaching the point of despair. She still refused to go to school. Writing of assignments and board preparations were done solely with the help of Tanya's class notes. Her outdoor sojourns were restricted to Doctor Madaan's clinic and to the physiotherapist.

She tried going for tuition with her hair combed in bangs that almost covered her eyes. But the sniggers from passers-by were just too many to ignore.

Papa and Mummy were worried about Asha's forthcoming board exams. It was quite evident that Asha's condition was distracting her. Instead of becoming more focused and concentrating on her studies, she was listless, refusing to even meet well-meaning teachers. But the final straw was when Asha gave up on her tuition classes after the first day itself.

'Papa, I can't do it. The teacher at that tuition class was passing comments behind my back, saying he would not be able to teach properly with me sitting in the class. Please don't make me go there. I promise I will study at home,' she appealed to her father, whom she could always rely on to make concessions.

Seeing her resistance, Mummy and Papa thought it best to insist that Asha acclimatize to real-world situations. That night, when they sat down for dinner, Mummy and Papa tried to lighten the mood by asking about the most over-the-top reaction that Asha had faced. When Asha did not respond, Mummy addressed the elephant in the room. 'Asha beta, you need to be a bit thick-skinned and put yourself out there. It is not healthy to lock yourself in like this,' she said.

Asha looked at Papa for support. He nodded instead in her mother's direction.

'Mummy's right, Asha. How will you prepare for the board exams if you don't meet your teachers? You should start meeting people socially too, okay?' he said gently.

This turn of events upset Asha to no end. 'I am just a problem for everyone,' she muttered angrily, walking away and plonking herself on the living room sofa. 'Happy to be alone,' she yelled again for emphasis. But much to her annoyance, Mummy and Papa were firm on this meet-and-greet-friends policy.

And so it started. The parade of 'well-meaning' visitors. Like Mummy's friend Radha Aunty, who began with 'Arre, poor girl. So young! How will she ever get married?'

Predictably, Asha seized the opportunity and generally acted difficult, hoping that her parents would eventually drop this preposterous idea of theirs. Luckily for her, just a few days later, the garrulous Shalini Aunty from F-block dropped by on a neighbourly visit with her daughter. After some small talk, she convinced Mummy and Asha to get into a huddle for a selfie. What she didn't tell them was that she would promptly share it on her Facebook wall.

When Asha saw it, she was livid and beyond consolation. 'I am now officially a freak show on social media, thanks to all of you. I hope you are happy,' she lashed out at Mummy and Papa in helpless anger.

Mummy was about to lecture her on toughening up to face the world, but Papa dissuaded her.

From her room, Asha overheard Papa telling Mummy, 'You have to be less pushy with her. Who knows? With the exam pressure and her accident, she might take some extreme steps.'

That stopped Mummy's 'tough love' exercises for a bit.

Good. Now I won't have to deal with all these horrid people, Asha thought to herself.

Much to Asha's relief, Mummy and Papa began discouraging visits from the friends and relatives that Asha was uncomfortable with.

'It's fine, beta. We now understand that this is not the best time for you to socialize,' Papa whispered, reassuring Asha as he made excuses to her Bua on the phone.

The result of this selective interaction was that Asha, now spared of the toxicity, was beginning to think with more clarity.

She realized that her accident and disappointment at missing out on the modelling audition had become a convenient excuse. It was quite evident that she needed to get her act together. School assignments and test papers needed urgent attention. And the weighing scales, too, were desperately hinting towards the need to exercise. Asha knew she had to get out there.

♡♡

Her first day of going for an evening stroll in the neighbourhood park had been predictable—a few horrified glances and a few sympathetic comments that were borderline offensive. Asha then reluctantly opted for an early morning jog in the park with a hooded T-shirt. Keeping her head down, she began jogging slowly at first.

A few minutes into the routine, Asha noticed a little girl of about nine or ten in a tattered dress who was sitting and reading a book in one corner of the park. The girl had a cleft lip. Asha stared at her and then suddenly realized with embarrassment that she was doing to the little girl exactly what others were doing to her. But the girl seemed oblivious to Asha's stare. Realizing she was being rude, Asha continued with her jog.

Over the next couple of laps of the park, Asha saw the little girl again and again. She hoped that the girl would look up and notice her. But each time, the girl was deep in concentration, reading her book.

On the fourth lap, when Asha was jogging past the girl's spot, she saw that a boy from the nearby *jhuggis* was trying to bully her about her cleft lip. Asha stopped and was about to step in and tell off the boy. But before she could do anything, Asha saw that the girl calmly stood up and smacked the boy hard on the face with her book. Then she chased the boy to the far end of the park. There, she leapt on him and brought him down to the ground. Then, finally, much to Asha's surprise, she proceeded to sit on him and would not let him up.

The boy protested loudly, but the girl smiled through her cleft lip at the hapless, pinned-down boy who was blubbering by now. She said, 'First, say that I'm the most beautiful girl in the world.'

The boy, crushed and helpless, reluctantly replied, 'Yes. Okay, baba. You are the most beautiful girl in the world.'

When the little girl finally got off him, the boy promptly sprang up and ran towards the jhuggis with his tail between his legs.

Asha just stood watching the entire incident, amused.

The little girl dusted the mud off her dress and walked off calmly towards the jhuggis as well.

Asha continued with her jog, making a mental note to chat with the little girl the next morning.

The next morning, when Asha went looking for the girl, she was nowhere to be seen. Asha approached the park guards and asked them if they had seen the girl that morning. The guards looked around and said that they didn't know about any little girl. Asha was the only person who entered the park so early in the morning.

Over the next few days, Asha looked out for the girl, but there was no sign of her. Asha even ventured into the jhuggis bordering the park to ask about the little girl with a cleft lip, but no one seemed to know her. It was as if the girl didn't exist.

Asha was intrigued. The little girl had disappeared as suddenly as she had appeared. As the weeks went by, Asha kept wondering about the little girl, and then a thought struck her one day. *The little girl must have been a fairy, sent to teach me a life lesson about counting one's blessings,* Asha thought.

'I ought to thank god I am alive instead of focusing on the state of my face,' Asha said aloud.

So, when Tanya told Asha about the school farewell party, she got a response that surprised and delighted her.

'Yes. I think I will give it a shot,' ventured Asha, feeling more cheerful than she had been for a long time.

Surprisingly, this time around, it was Mummy and Papa who felt uncertain about Asha venturing into a party-type social situation.

'I am not sure if this would be the right occasion for you to step out, beta . . . selfies, drinking and boisterous party behaviour . . . a bit extreme and uncontrolled it will be, na?' Papa said, reminding her of the fallout of the Shalini-Aunty episode.

'Haan . . . *aur abhi tak zyada* improvement *bhi nahin hua hai.* Asha, why do you want to go to a party looking like this? You never know who will make a rude comment and send you into depression,' quizzed Dadi, oblivious to the disapproving glares from Mummy and Papa.

'Of course, I reserve the right to back out if I don't feel up to it, right?' Asha countered, suddenly feeling a little unsure.

Of her friends, Tanya, the old faithful, was over the moon at the idea of having her bestie back in school with her. It was fun to talk about something other than their upcoming board exams. But other buddies, Priya and Rachna, were not all that enthusiastic, although they did not overtly express themselves.

Every single day leading up to the big event, Priya and Rachna called to check if Asha had changed her mind. Tanya had bullied them into cooperating, but they too had laid down their terms. 'Let's be very clear. We are not going to leave the party early if Asha has an emotional meltdown or something. Okay?' Priya and Rachna chorused to Tanya when she disclosed her plans for the grand entry the four would make at the party.

'Just half an hour, okay? But you stay! I don't want to be a killjoy and drag you away from the fun,' Asha told Tanya nervously as they got into the car on the day of the party. Papa had rather generously assigned the office car and driver to his darling daughter for the entire day!

Finally, Asha's moment of reckoning arrived. There she was, all dressed up in the elegant green Zara dress, with Tanya as her knight in shining armour for the night. With some help from Tanya, Asha had strategically taped and covered her unblinking eye with her hair stylishly drawn over half her face.

The school looked all festive, with the auditorium decorated with festoons and posters. Loud music and the gathering of excited students did little to ease Asha's nervousness, and she was thankful for her friend's company. After a few minutes of small talk and emotional hugs, they all went into the auditorium. The customary speeches and announcements were made by the principal, who, after some exam advice and a few cheeky jokes about the students, left them to enjoy the party with their class teachers and classmates.

As her favourite songs began to play, Asha forgot all about the twist to her face and the half-an-hour time limit she had set for herself. She and Tanya just grooved away.

One of the guys from her class, whom Asha and Tanya made fun of and called 'Bhukkad' behind his back, walked up to Asha and started dancing with her. *Shit! I don't even know his real name,* thought Asha. She was nervous as hell now and looked around for Tanya, who was busy chatting with a cute-looking chap and totally ignoring Asha.

As if reading Asha's mind, the boy said, 'I know you call me Bhukkad, but my name is Sandesh, and my friends call me Sandy.'

Asha went beetroot red. Luckily, her hair was hiding most of her face.

'Hey, you have lovely hair. But why do you use it to cover your face?' Sandy asked Asha.

'Some problem with my eye,' she hastily explained. She then cracked a few self-conscious jokes about her crooked, lopsided smile and how she was not taking any chances with winning the Miss Pleasant Personality of the Year award.

Asha had imagined that Sandy would move away to a group of pretty girls close by, but he stayed and prattled on about the forthcoming exams and his favourite subjects. In fact, some of Sandy's friends joined him, too. As did Tanya, Priya and Rachna.

The boys and the girls danced away till the 'Cinderella Hour' and exchanged numbers before saying their goodbyes.

By now, Asha had tied up her hair and forgotten all about her unblinking eye and twisted mouth.

Much to everyone's surprise, the school farewell party drew to an end without any of the anticipated melodrama or crisis—unless Priya tripping and falling while dancing in her ridiculously high heels counted. Tanya had got herself a date, and Asha had managed an entire evening without getting her feathers ruffled by comments or stares! It was indeed a night to remember.

A couple of days later, Asha went to Dr Madaan for her weekly check-up, and he was surprised as hell.

'Asha beti, you look much better.' He checked her reports from the week before and raised a quizzical eyebrow, 'Definitely a significant improvement. What happened?' he asked, somewhat incredulously.

In her mind, Asha pictured the little girl in the park with a cleft lip.

'I just started seeing myself as the most beautiful girl in the world,' Asha said, flashing a bright, lopsided smile.

THIS ISN'T FAIR

Santhini Govindan

'When will Ammamma be here?' Fourteen-year-old Shreya asked her mother eagerly as she ate her breakfast. 'I can't wait for her visit! I am dying to tell her that after hours of hard practice, I beat the competition and made it to the under-sixteen school athletics team. Do you think that she will be happy to hear about it, Amma?'

'Ammamma will be here in less than a week,' Amma replied, 'and I'm sure she will be very happy to hear about your achievement.'

Shreya was pleased. Her grandmother was her favourite person, and she always looked forward to her visits because Ammamma was loving and indulgent, and she always made such a fuss about her. Of course, her visits were also delightful because she was a superb cook.

Her grandmother always arrived with numerous, odd-looking pieces of luggage, filled with tins and bottles and *dabbas* crammed with homemade goodies. Shreya smacked her lips, remembering the aromas that floated up in the air as Ammamma opened each of her bags. She would make and bring them mouth-watering ghee-drenched sweets, tangy savouries—pickles made from mangoes grown in her own garden—and delicious, gooey jackfruit preserve that she made annually when the fruit was in season in Kerala.

Ammamma was also a skilled needlewoman. When Shreya got her first mobile phone, her grandmother had made her a small but unique phone sling bag. Everyone oohed and aahed over it, because it had been crocheted in fine gold and silver thread and looked like an expensive designer bag that no one else had. Ammamma liked to knit, too. On her last visit, Shreya had persuaded her to knit a little striped sweater for their dachshund, Dobby, to wear during cold, wintry days.

'I wonder what Ammamma will bring me this time,' Shreya wondered as she walked to the school bus stop. 'I will be thrilled if she has been able to knit the rainbow-coloured shrug I saw in that magazine and showed her the last time we went to visit her. I've never seen anything like it in any of the branded clothing stores. It looked so smart—I can use it to dress up so many of my outfits. Plus, it stands in support of the queer, and I love that!'

A few days later, when Shreya came home from school, her grandmother had already arrived. Full of smiles as usual, Ammamma hugged Shreya warmly.

'What goodies have you brought for me?' Shreya asked impatiently, getting to the point straightaway. Her grandmother chuckled and reached for the roomy, battered leather bag that she always packed her food items in.

'Here's your favourite,' she said, taking out a tin filled with brown squares.

'Ooh, it's condensed milk toffee!' Shreya squealed excitedly, grabbing two pieces immediately. As Amma took the tin away, Ammamma brought out two more containers filled with gooey banana halwa and sweet *rawa* laddus loaded with cashew nuts and raisins.

'You can't have so many sweets now, Shreya,' Amma said firmly, before Shreya could help herself to a few more. Shreya grimaced and ate a few tapioca chips instead. She watched intently and expectantly as Ammamma opened her suitcase.

'I knitted something for you,' she said.

Shreya whooped with excitement. 'I have been waiting to see what you would make for me this time!'

When Ammamma held up a colourful knitted shrug, Shreya could barely contain her excitement. She excitedly grabbed it from her grandmother and slipped it on over her school uniform. Then she pirouetted around in it, squealing with delight. 'This shrug looks even better than the one I saw in your magazine!' she exclaimed. 'I will have fun teaming it with different outfits.'

Ammamma beamed. 'I'm glad you like it. It's the first time I have knitted a shrug. I've brought something else also—something you will need now that you are a teenager.'

'What is it? Show me,' said Shreya eagerly. She loved presents, and her grandmother's handmade presents were the best. She dipped into her suitcase again and brought out two tightly capped bottles.

'What's in those?' Shreya asked curiously. Before she could reply, Shreya snatched one of the bottles from her grandmother's hand. She quickly uncapped it and sniffed it. But as soon as she had done this, she scrunched up her nose and handed the bottle back to her grandmother. 'Eeww!' Shreya said with a grimace. 'That smells weird! What on earth is it? If it smells like that, I'm pretty sure that it won't taste good either.'

Ammamma laughed heartily. 'It's not meant to be eaten, Shreya! It's an *ubtan*.'

'Ubtan? What on earth is that?'

'An ubtan is an ancient ayurvedic recipe made using herbs and natural ingredients. It's a potion that you must apply to your skin. It will make your skin healthy and glowing.'

Shreya looked at her grandmother in genuine puzzlement. 'But my skin is quite healthy.' She stretched out her lanky arms. 'Look!' she said earnestly. 'It may not be glowing, but my skin looks quite all right to me.'

Ammamma sighed. 'I think I brought these ubtans just in time,' she said with a stern expression. 'In fact, when I saw you, I was surprised to see the colour of your skin,' she said frankly to Shreya. 'You are as dark as a crow, and I don't think that your burnt skin looks attractive at all.'

Shreya was taken aback to hear these scathing words, especially from her beloved grandmother. She brushed them aside and said, 'Ammamma, wait till you hear what I have to tell you!' She was sure her grandmother would be happy and proud when she heard the news. 'I have been chosen for my school's under-sixteen athletics team. I am in the 100-metres sprint and in the relay race, too! Isn't that exciting?'

'Exciting? No! You will be playing sports. Dashing about in the hot sun hasn't helped your looks at all. Luckily, my *vaidyan*, Ravindran Nair, is a magician. If you

THIS ISN'T FAIR

rub the special ubtans that he has created on your skin regularly, you will soon get rid of that ugly tan, and your skin will become much fairer. Your amma must have told you that there's a big wedding coming up in our family next month—all our relatives will be there! Don't you want everyone to say how pretty and fair you are?'

'That's it? Is that all you have to say about my exciting news?' Shreya exclaimed furiously, her eyes flashing with anger. 'Aren't you even going to congratulate me on getting into the school athletics team? It was a herculean task, and I had to work very hard.' Her disappointment at her grandmother's reaction was evident.

'I don't want my skin to be fairer; I like it just the way it is,' Shreya retorted mutinously after a pause. '. . . and I really enjoy playing sports and running around in the sun! You know, everyone else thought it was a big deal when I told them I would be representing my school in the inter-city school sports event. I'm going to do my best to win a medal in my events.' Shreya scowled at her grandmother, who looked decidedly displeased after hearing Shreya's retorts. But she was made of sterner stuff and was not ready to give up her fairness campaign.

'I know that you are a good athlete, Shreya. We are all proud of you,' Ammamma said evenly, trying to adopt a conciliatory tone. 'But you have to take care of your appearance, too. You will look much prettier if your skin is fairer. Now, if you had got your mother's complexion instead of your father's, you wouldn't have had to worry at all, but alas!' She clicked her tongue loudly in dismay. 'You got Kumar's complexion,' Ammamma ended disappointedly.

Shreya received this remark in shocked silence. Then, she drew herself up to her full height and exclaimed loudly and indignantly, 'I think my father is very handsome!'

'Of course, he's handsome,' Ammamma replied, 'But he's dark-skinned too. It doesn't matter in his case, of course, because he's a man and a very clever one, too. But you are a girl, Shreya. And you will find it most unhelpful if you don't have fair skin.'

'Says who?' Shreya asked hotly. She was upset and angry that her grandmother, instead of praising her and being proud of her athletic prowess, as she had expected, was only interested in criticizing the colour of her skin. Shreya's eyes glistened with tears. She stamped her foot. 'I don't care what you think, Ammamma! Shreya declared. 'I am not going to rub that foul-smelling goo on my body to become fair! I don't want to waste my energy trying to make my skin fairer! I want to become a scientist and an athletics champion!'

'An athletics champion?' Ammamma's voice rose in a dismayed shriek, and she looked horrified. 'Good grief! I suppose that means running about more in the hot sun! What will you look like then? Your skin will look and feel rough, like burnt toast!'

She turned around and glared at her daughter. 'This is all your fault, Latha! You should have stopped Kumar from encouraging Shreya to take up athletics! Now she has no interest in doing anything but dashing around in the scorching heat! And see how stubborn and argumentative she has become!'

Shreya did not wait to hear her mother's reply to this remark. She ran to her room and slammed the door shut.

That night, Shreya wasn't her usual talkative self at the dinner table. When Ammamma tried to draw her into the conversation, she responded grimly and in monosyllables. She didn't even go to her grandmother's room to say goodnight and chat with her as she used to earlier.

The next morning, as Shreya and her mother walked to the school bus stop, Shreya asked, 'Amma, why does Ammamma think that it is more important to have fair skin than being good at sports? I don't get it. You always tell me that it's important to work hard towards achieving goals. I worked and gave it my all to get into the athletics team. I pushed my limits. I thought Ammamma would be proud of me, but she said that I am as dark as a crow. All she seems to be concerned with is how to make me fairer.' Shreya's voice mirrored her disappointment, resentment and unhappiness.

'You know, Shreya, your ammamma grew up at a time when girls did not have any of the opportunities that you have today, especially not in sports,' Amma said gently. 'She doesn't mean to hurt you. She's trying to help you in the only way she knows. Even when you were just a baby, she had brought a whole lot of ubtans and *leps* to apply on your body. I did give in then. Do you remember? I suppose you don't. Then, when you were seven or eight, she brought some *kashayam*, a herbal tonic of sorts, for you to drink, but I put my foot down then.' Amma sighed, then said, 'Give her a little time. I think she'll eventually understand . . . and things will get better.'

Shreya smiled wanly at her mother.

'I hope so,' she said uncertainly. 'I don't remember that Ammamma—the one who got herbal pastes and concoctions. I remember the Ammamma who brings toffees, sweets and handmade things. And I *really* miss her!'

But things did not get better soon. In fact, two days later, the situation got worse. Ammamma and Amma decided to go shopping to buy clothes for the

THIS ISN'T FAIR

family wedding, and Shreya was, of course, part of this expedition.

Ammamma was in her element when they entered the silk-sari shop, and Shreya watched wide-eyed as dozens of shimmering, brightly coloured sarees were opened and displayed before her. Ruby-red, jade-green and turquoise blue—each sari was more striking than the next. After she had finished choosing saris, Ammamma told Shreya, 'I am going to buy you a *pattu-pavadai*. Choose one.'

Shreya pulled out a dark green silk from the pile of skirt pieces. 'I like this one,' she said eagerly to Ammamma. 'It's the same colour as the leaves of my favourite mango tree in your garden!'

Ammamma frowned. 'But it's not at all suitable for you, dear,' she said. 'It's a dark colour and will make your skin look even darker.' She held up a bright canary-yellow silk. 'Look at this one! It is a light colour that is much more suitable for your dusky skin tone. Isn't it pretty?'

'No! It's not! I hate yellow,' Shreya said rudely. 'I will not wear a colour that I dislike.' Her tone was firm and decisive.

'Well then, I'm definitely not buying that dark green pavadai for you.' Her voice rising sharply, Ammamma matched her granddaughter's stubbornness.

As Shreya glared at her grandmother, she yelled, 'This ISN'T FAIR!' She was nearly in tears.

Amma quickly told the shopkeeper, 'We'll come back to buy the pavadai another day.' She hurriedly ushered her angry mother and daughter out of the store, and there was an icy silence in the autorickshaw as they went back home.

In the following week, Shreya had extra athletics practice after school, as the inter-school sports meet was just days away. When she came home after practice, Shreya avoided Ammamma and stayed in her own room with Dobby. Ammamma noticed this and was hurt, of course. Shreya was ignoring what she believed was sensible and useful advice. Once, she walked into her granddaughter's room, but then she quietly stepped away: Shreya was doing her stretches. Ammamma soon found her anger and resentment melting as she watched her young granddaughter throw herself fully into preparations for her sports meet.

What had it been like when I was fourteen? Ammamma wondered wistfully. She remembered being athletic and competitive, too. In fact, she delighted in beating her brothers in the impromptu swimming competitions they had in the *kulam*, the pond in which the boys bathed daily. But when her grandmother had found out that she was swimming with boys . . . there was no escaping her wrath!

As she thought about her arguments with Shreya, Ammamma realized remorsefully that she had been

THIS ISN'T FAIR

doing to Shreya exactly what her elders had done to her. Sighing, she looked around herself. It had been more than sixty years, and here she was, harsh and rigid with her own granddaughter. She inhaled deeply—she knew what she could do to set things right.

Finally, the all-important day of the inter-city school sports meet dawned. Shreya was quite nervous. 'I have butterflies in my stomach,' she confessed to her father as he drove her to school.

'You have practised very sincerely. Now just do the best you can,' came his reassuring reply. 'Amma and I will be there to cheer you on proudly!'

As the athletes took their marks before the 100-metre sprint event, Shreya felt that her heart was pounding so loudly that everyone standing nearby could probably hear it. Then the starting pistol sounded, and the runners were off with a bang.

How Shreya ran! The crowds erupted into a jubilant cheer as she sprinted across the finish line. Shreya finished second and won a silver medal! As she got ready to ascend the winner's podium and receive her medal, Shreya's eyes scanned the crowd, looking for her parents. She spotted them and waved, and then her eyes widened—Ammamma was seated between her parents! And she was beaming and smiling broadly. When Shreya received her medal, her grandmother stood up and clapped loudly. When Shreya's team won the gold medal in the relay race, she again leapt out of her chair to cheer and applaud.

'You ran so well,' Ammamma said to Shreya when they were driving back home. 'I was so proud of you! Perhaps you will be the next Payyoli Express!' *I love you and I am so, so proud of you*, thought Ammamma.

'Payyoli Express? What's that?' *Thank you for coming, Ammamma. It means the world to me*, thought Shreya.

The two sat there next to each other in the car, smiling at each other in silence. It was only when Dad cleared his throat that Ammamma said, 'Payyoli Express is P.T. Usha's nickname. You must know about her.'

Shreya beamed. 'Of course! She was one of India's finest track and field athletes. P.T. Usha was only sixteen years old when she competed at the 1980 Moscow Olympic Games! Isn't that amazing?' Shreya wanted to tell Ammamma more. Instead, she leaned to the side and rested her head on her grandmother's shoulder, who immediately wrapped her arms around this child who was growing into a fine young woman.

Shreya's father looked at the two in the rear-view mirror, and his eyes crinkled. He glanced at his wife. Shreya's mom was smiling, looking straight ahead.

Ammamma kissed the top of Shreya's head and said quietly, 'Next time you come to Kerala, let's go to the sports academy that P.T. Usha set up to train girls in athletics at Kozhikode.'

Shreya sat up straight. 'Really, Ammamma? Can we do that?!'

Ammamma looked at Shreya, all bright-eyed and bushy-tailed. *I'm sorry that I was so fixated about skin colour and you getting darker*, Ammamma thought, but didn't say those words. Instead, she held Shreya's face in her hands, kissed her brows and said, 'You do the things you love, *kutty*. You keep running and having fun. Whether you win or not, if I am here, I will come for every event of yours, and I will cheer you the loudest!'

That night, Shreya went to Ammamma's room, like she used to, to hear her stories. Before Shreya could speak, her grandmother put a brown paper bag into Shreya's hands.

'Here's a little gift for you,' she said. 'You really deserve it for your wonderful performance today!'

Shreya opened the bag, and a silk skirt piece tumbled out. It shone in the light—it was as green as the leaves on a mango tree.

SINKING INTO MY SKIN

Rajani Thindiath

When music sweeps me under, the rhythm, the beats pulse through my veins, and I dance with abandon. Every leap, every swirl is joyously graceful. The choreography is spontaneous . . . in my mind's eye. But self-consciousness and I, we are best buds. That is why when Ms Retta calls for dancers for our school's annual day, I kind of slump back. They tend to pick the toppers or their favourites, anyway. And I . . . well, I get uneasy pushing myself forward, calling attention to myself like some of my super-confident classmates do.

'Okay, eighth graders,' Ms Retta announces. 'I want everyone to head to the main hall for selection. We'll play some music, and I want all of you to dance. Yes, all of you. No complaints or excuses, please. We will pick those who are suitable for this dance.' And with that, Ms Retta marches off.

Excitement buzzes as we head to the hall. I look around and realize that mostly everyone's just like me. We all want to be in the spotlight, to be the chosen ones. But we are too timid to put ourselves out there. But to dance when everyone's dancing? This we can do!

The music starts, and we all just shuffle around a little self-consciously. We catch each other's eyes and giggle. Soon, we begin to laugh as we dance our hearts out. And guess what? I am selected!

'Okay, each of those selected will come forward individually and showcase a dance item. Pick anything you like,' calls out Ms Retta.

I would love to groove to one of the popular numbers, but I know my steps will fall into a loop. They tend to do that when I am outside my head, so conscious of the watching eyes that my mind blanks out. So, I am sticking to one of the short classical dances that I have performed since I was four.

My heart starts to pound. Classical dances are performed barefoot. Keeping my knee-high socks on is sure to send me slipping across the smooth tiled floor. But if I remove my socks, they will all see my legs—my legs with dry, wrinkled skin that has formed cracks which look like the scales on a crocodile's back or remind one of those photos of arid fields where fissures run long and deep.

But everyone is waiting. A toss-up between removing my socks or not dancing? That's a no-brainer. I slip out of my socks, wishing my pinafore were long enough to cover my legs.

The music starts, and I begin to dance. I focus my eyes on my hand movements, as I have been taught. I feel stiff and disjointed. I sense the eyes on my legs, the appalled stares focused on the white, dry flakes contrasting with my dark skin. I can feel my skin shrink away from those eyes and wither under their disgust.

Gradually, my body catches the rhythm, and I flow with the music, feeling like sparkling dust motes swirling through the sunlit air. I come to a halt to enthusiastic applause from everyone, and bubbles of joy fizz through me. The teachers look happy and are clapping, too. Then, Ms Gar calls out, 'You should really put moisturizer on your legs, Raaga. They are very dry.'

The smile freezes on my face. I desperately try not to look around, quite sure that everyone is now looking at, whispering about and pitying my scaly legs. I mumble something about forgetting to moisturize and hurriedly pull my socks on. I am too embarrassed to admit that my family cannot afford luxuries like moisturizers.

Then, Ms Dhran approaches me and says, 'You are selected, Raaga. You have a natural grace about you.' I beam my thanks, but then she pats my shoulder sympathetically and continues in a whisper, 'Avoid dark-coloured clothes for your dance, though. They won't suit you. You could try applying cucumber, you know. I've heard this *baba* recommend it for fairer skin.'

'Sure, ma'am. Thank you, ma'am,' I blurt out, wretchedly holding on to my smile, feeling it stretch my skin as if it would tear right across my face. This is advice I have heard before. Every time I go shopping, I tend to pick either white or some shade of brown or olive green. Browns and olive greens are like camouflage. They don't call attention to my darkness.

I watch Ms Dhran walk away and feel my throat clamming up. I am too scared to look around to check who had overheard the horrible exchange. That's when an arm lands around my shoulder, and my friends Shivani and Renuka come up beside me. 'Raaga! Great going, ya! You danced so beautifully!'

'Thanks, ya.' I smile and then grimace, 'But I have to figure out my sari. I hate that I can't wear all colours. Fair people like you can wear what they like.'

'Hardly!' Shivani snorts. 'Even fair people can't wear certain colours. For example, pale shades tend to wash me out. As for you, you are beautiful! Why are you worried?'

I smile, grateful for her attempt at making me feel better. But of course, she doesn't really mean it. Beautiful? Who, me? No way! No one's ever called me that. The most I have got from folks at home is that I have pretty eyes.

How many times have I heard the phrase *nalla niram illa* in Malayalam? Any dark-skinned person is just not 'fair enough'. My younger, fairer sibling is always the ideal. She is the beautiful one with her rosy skin, silky hair, long lashes and gorgeous eyes.

'You know,' Renuka interrupts my thoughts casually. 'You look like this actor from the sixties. She is a friend of my mother's.'

Now, I inwardly roll my eyes. Right! I look like an actor. They are really going overboard with their attempts to make me feel good.

But Shivani continues, 'You are right, Renuka. And you know what, Raaga? You should really avoid browns in your clothes. What are you trying to do? Fade into the background? You should try bright yellows, fuchsia, oranges and bright blues. They will make that dark chocolate skin of yours pop and glow!'

Yeah, that's what I want. For my dark skin to pop and glow like I am some neon sign. I'd just look gaudy. No, thanks. But their well-meaning cheer brightens my day.

I enjoyed dancing, got selected and have kind friends. What more could I want?

♡♡

That evening, I am getting ready to go out when my hands reach for my lime-green top, which I love but rarely wear. It makes my dark skin stand out, and I am intensely uncomfortable imagining all the sympathetic and, sometimes, taunting glances that will come my way. But since I am on a roll now, I decide not to think about it.

As I brush my hair, I observe my hands in the mirror. They don't look like they belong to a fourteen-year-old. They are full of lines and wrinkles, like the hands of my great-grandmom. A classmate had once looked at my hands and asked me, giggling, if my mother made me do all the dishes at home. I felt like Cinderella that day, sorry for myself, even though I don't have to lift a finger at home. But today, I watch the evening sunlight pour through my hands, turning the pale skin stretching between my fingers red. I turn my palms up and down, looking at the contrast between the dark skin at the back of my hands and the pale skin of my palms.

Why am I so dark and wrinkled? I stare at the mango tree I love opposite my window, its leaves fluttering and shining green in the warm sunlight. I love looking at the whorls and lines on the bark. So many seasons and so many years the tree has seen. Then, I suddenly look down at my hands. Whorls and lines there, too. I have never looked at my hands quite in this manner. Now that I am looking at them, I have never ever seen hands like mine. So, what if they are wrinkled and dry? *If I can't be fair and lovely, I will be unique,* I decide.

I like the comparison to the bark of the mango tree. I don't know why, but it makes me feel good. As if I am special, like my great-grandmother. With a start, I realize she is dark like me. *Why have I never noticed this before?* To me, she always looks radiant.

Buoyed by the thought, I search the web to see if there is anything I can do for my dry skin. Sometimes, it gets so dry that it itches madly. Scratching just makes it worse, and the cracks bleed.

I am not expecting much, and a lot of advice is just plain fishy. I go in search of legit sources associated with medical schools or hospitals, and I am astounded. I read an article that advises against using soap. *Chee*! How can anyone be clean without using soap? The article goes on to say that extremely dry skin does not produce natural oil and soap sucks out any moisture in the skin, making it itch. A homemade remedy is to leave curds out at night, apply it to the skin before a bath the next day, let it dry, rub it out and wash off with water. I am skeptical about these suggestions but decide to give them a try.

I have left out the curd, but when I apply it in the bathroom the next day, it is rather smelly. In fact, it stinks up the bathroom so badly that it reminds me of an awful school visit to a dairy factory. But my stars! The amount of time it takes to rub the dried curd out of my skin! Though my skin feels better afterwards, I cross this experiment off. There's no way I am doing this every day. Forget pitying my scaly skin; I will just send everyone scurrying with my stink explosion!

Next, I try to go without soap, especially on my limbs, where my skin is the driest and . . . the itching stops! Now this, I can do. Over the next couple of weeks, a little bud of confidence unfurls in me with the realization that my problems are not insurmountable. There are tips and ways to get around them. I just need to ask the right questions to figure out simple solutions to my problems on my own. Isn't the Internet wonderful?

As I start to take care of myself, the itchiness fades, and I start feeling better and happier. There is a new energy when I practise my steps at home. I watch my fingers, hands and body move, enjoying their grace. Wrinkled or not, dancing makes my body come alive like nothing else.

♡♡

When the annual day dawns, I am super excited as Mom drapes a yellow half-sari with a red border around me. It is 'half' because it falls just below the knees for ease of dancing. Yellow does make me glow, or perhaps it is just this delight fizzing through me. At school, my smiles flow freely, and I bustle around the room, helping others with their make-up.

I am feeling so good that I am hardly disturbed when someone spills *alta* on my sari. The red ink that is used to paint the tips of a dancer's fingers and toes is splashed over the front folds of my costume. I wash it off, figuring that my sari has enough time to dry off while I await my turn to go on stage.

And then it is time. The spotlight is on me, as I have always wanted it to be. Everyone is watching, but this time, I feel a wave of exhilaration wash over me. I begin to dance, and, for the first time, I am aware of my body, my movements and the sheer release and exuberance I find in dance . . . beyond all the eyes watching me.

But thoughts—painful and uncomfortable—prick at me. 'Dark', 'scaly', 'flaky', 'disgusting'—these words flash through me. They have always been a part of me, and they don't want to let go. I lose my focus, and panic strikes! My mind blanks out . . . The steps! What are the next steps?

But even as my mind scatters, my body remembers. Hours and hours of practice have so drilled the steps into my muscle memory that they flow seamlessly, one following the other almost automatically. My heart flutters like a trapped bird as I let go of my panic and dive into the flow.

This is my chance, my moment. The drumbeat of my heart seems to thud in my head, whooshing down to thrum in the soles of my tapping feet.

Thud. I hold on to the anchor I have found in myself. *Thud.* I am unique. *Thud.* No one can take that away from me. *Thud.* And then, my entire being flies even as I sink into the beats. I am lost in the way my fingers arch and curve and my body sways, lost in the euphoria of the rhythm. The applause that comes at the end of my dance, the proud smiles on the faces of my parents and teachers—that is the icing on my cake.

The curtains close, and Ms Retta approaches. I hear my heartbeat in my ears as I brace for some new, well-meaning comment on my skin. Then, I decide I am too happy at this moment. *Whatever the teacher says, I will shrug it off and move on.*

'You know, Raaga, all the teachers watching you were talking about how beautiful your movements are. Do you practise and perfect each gesture in front of the mirror?' Ms Retta laughs.

My heart soars. They did not talk about my skin! A smile blooms inside my heart and spreads all over my body. I feel so light, I could float. So full of bubbles of light sparkling through me that I am sure my joy radiates outwards, brushing everyone around me with the brightest, sweetest touch.

ACKNOWLEDGEMENTS

My thanks to all the people who made this book possible:

To Lakshmi Priya of Pachyderm Tales, who dreamt of doing this book. Thank you for thinking that a book on body positivity for teenagers really needs to be done. Thank you for taking all the steps to set it up.

To the fifteen authors who quietly sent me the stories without even asking what they would get paid and without a ghost of a contract. Thank you for your trust and patience, each one of you.

Thank you Mallika Dua for the fierce, moving, powerfully-validating foreword. Your words add to the beauty of this book.

Thank you to Tanvi Bhat, who threw me my first line of hope when door after door was shutting. This book may not have been born if you hadn't listened to me that day and helped me with what you did.

ACKNOWLEDGEMENTS

A big thanks to my wonderful editor, Sushmita Chatterjee, who appeared godsent, like an oxygen mask, when the cabin pressure dropped. I don't know what I would have done without you.

Thank you, Shabari Choudhury, for your remarkable editing skills and teaching me a lesson in professionalism. Your painstaking editing and obtaining the consent of each contributor for every correction remind me that there are awesome people out there.

So many people helped me during this book with friendship, generosity and encouragement—Mrudula, Ramya, Juggie, Vikram.

Thank you, Kripa, for being that friend, my forever sounding board, and for always making sense in this nonsense world. I love your insights about everything. Where would I be without our dialogues?

I am grateful for my kids, upon whom I foist stories by reading passages aloud and seeking their opinions with very little notice.

Thank you, Vani Ramchandani, for letting me use your story and patiently letting me lean on you despite your adolescent ennui.

And yay to Priyanka Paul for agreeing to do the cover. My dream of us doing books together is yet to be fulfilled, but this is a start.

CONTRIBUTORS

Aditi De is a 24/7 dreamer. She believes in a child-centric world, in words, in travelling solo to make friends, and in deep conversations. She has written fourteen books to date.

Anuja Chandramouli is a bestselling and award-winning author. A new-age Indian classicist, she has published twelve books across mythology, historical fiction and fantasy genres.

Harshikaa Udasi is usually found in the company of children, reading and narrating stories. Her hair has often been ridiculed, but she has learnt over time to take pride in who she is and what she has.

Janani Balaji's stories and poetry on gender bias, mental health and queer rights are part of distinguished anthologies. *Thinking of You*, her story in verse, is a powerful narrative on depression.

Nandini Nayar is the author of over seventy-five books for children of all ages. For more information about Nandini Nayar, please visit her website www.nandininayar.in.

Neha Singh is a Mumbai-based author, theatre practitioner and women's rights activist. She was chosen as one of the hundred most influential women in the world by BBC for her campaign 'Why Loiter?'

Priyanka Sinha Jha has authored the books *Supertraits of Superstars* (self-help) and *Folktales From Bollywood* (short stories). She's been the editor of the *Hindustan Times (Café)* and magazines such as the *Screen* and *Society*.

Rajani Thindiath was the editor-in-chief of Tinkle Comics for a decade and is the creator of the *SuperWeirdos* and *YogYodhas* series. She was a juror at the British Fantasy Awards (2022) and the Publishing Next Awards (2023 and 2021). For more information about her, do visit her website: https://rajanithindiath.wixsite.com/my-site-1.

CONTRIBUTORS

Ratna Manucha is an academician, storyteller, poet, columnist and author of fact, fiction and textbooks for children and young adults. She lives, dreams and writes in Dehra Dun, her happy place.

Santhini Govindan is an award-winning author of over fifty children's books. Her stories and poems appear in over a hundred literature readers and are used in schools across India and Asia.

Shals Mahajan is a writer, activist, layabout, part feline, somewhat hooman, genderqueer fellow. Their published works include *Timmi in Tangles*, *Timmi and Rizu*, *Reva and Prisha* and *No Outlaws in the Gender Galaxy* (co-author).

Smita Vyas Kumar has been a serial entrepreneur for most of her working life after acquiring an MBA from IIM Bangalore. She is now a full-time writer, poet and amateur artist.

Suha Riyaz Khopatkar is an architect, author, award-winning illustrator, educator and art-based therapy practitioner from Mumbai. Her work focuses on pursuing self-awareness and personal development through music, drama and art.

Vibha Batra is an author, poet, adperson, graphic novelist, lyricist, translator, playwright, scriptwriter, travel writer, columnist and speaker. She has published twenty-seven books, many of which have won prestigious awards, bestseller tags and readers' hearts.

Vidya Nesarikar is a children's writer and storyteller. In 2023, she was a finalist for the Scholastic Asian Book Award. She writes regularly for the *Young World*, the children's supplement of the *Hindu*. You can contact her at sodapopstories@gmail.com.

Read More in Penguin

BIG MISTAKE

A label-defying collection for every young adult

Insecurities and assurances, conflict and solidarity, fearfulness and courage—the personal histories, stories and #ownvoices in this anthology cover a lot of ground in just a few pages. Let them spark conversations on love, identity, disability, family, body positivity, ambition and other tough stuff.

After all, no matter how old we get, growing up can feel like one big mistake.

Includes fiction, non-fiction and poetry from: *Saina Nehwal, Japleen Pasricha, Jane de Suza, Andaleeb Wajid, Anusha Misra, Kautuk Srivastava, Parvati Sharma, Neha Singh, Nandana Dev Sen, Nikhil Taneja, Hannah Lalhlanpuii* and *Sonaksha Iyengar*.

Read More in Penguin

UNDER THE BAKUL TREE

Mrinal Kalita
Translated from the Assamese by
Partha Pratim Goswami

An award-winning literary masterpiece from Assam

When Ashim, the gifted class topper—hailed as the 'jewel'—suddenly drops out of school, everyone is surprised. Nirmal, his classmate and academic rival, is deeply troubled by Ashim's scholastic downfall and decides to investigate. As he fights his own demons, Nirmal uncovers the tangled layers of Ashim's troubles and a friendship as pristine as the bakul flower blooms in the tender hearts of two innocent boys. While systemic corruption, a failed education system and ecological destruction play out in the background, an idealistic and imaginative mentor helps the boys navigate the burdens of adolescence, academic pressure and psychological trauma.

A heart-warming coming-of-age tale celebrating friendship, hope and determination, *Under the Bakul Tree* is one of the finest young adult novels to emerge from the regional canvas of India and is an invaluable addition to its rich literary landscape.

Scan QR code to access the
Penguin Random House India website